THE ROVER BOYS ON THE GREAT LAKES

Or, The Secret Of The Island Cave

ARTHUR M. WINFIELD
(Edward Stratemeyer)

1st WORLD LIBRARY
Literary Society

The Rover Boys on the Great Lakes

Arthur M. Winfield

© 1st World Library, 2007
PO Box 2211
Fairfield, IA 52556
www.1stworldlibrary.com
First Edition

LCCN: 2007923752

Softcover ISBN: 978-1-4218-4235-6
Hardcover ISBN: 978-1-4218-4137-3
eBook ISBN: 978-1-4218-4333-9

Purchase *"The Rover Boys on the Great Lakes"*
as a traditional bound book at:
www.1stWorldLibrary.com/purchase.asp?ISBN=978-1-4218-4235-6

1st World Library is a literary, educational organization
dedicated to:

- Creating a free internet library of downloadable ebooks

- Hosting writing competitions and offering book
publishing scholarships.

Interested in more 1st World Library books?
contact: literacy@1stworldlibrary.com
Check us out at: www.1stworldlibrary.com

1st World Library Literary Society

Giving Back to the World

"If you want to work on the core problem, it's early school literacy."

- James Barksdale, former CEO of Netscape

"No skill is more crucial to the future of a child, or to a democratic and prosperous society, than literacy."

- Los Angeles Times

Literacy... means far more than learning how to read and write... The aim is to transmit... knowledge and promote social participation."

- UNESCO

"Literacy is not a luxury, it is a right and a responsibility. If our world is to meet the challenges of the twenty-first century we must harness the energy and creativity of all our citizens."

- President Bill Clinton

"Parents should be encouraged to read to their children, and teachers should be equipped with all available techniques for teaching literacy, so the varying needs and capacities of individual kids can be taken into account."

- Hugh Mackay

CONTENTS

INTRODUCTION

MY DEAR BOYS: This volume, "The Rover Boys on the Great Lakes," is a complete story in itself, but forms the fifth volume of the Rover Boys Series for Young Americans.

When first I started this series with "The Rover Boys at School," I had no idea of extending the line beyond three or four volumes. But the second book, "The Rover Boys on the Ocean," immediately called for a third, "The Rover Boys in the Jungle," and this finished, many boys wanted to know what would happen next, and so I must needs give them "The Rover Boys Out West." Still they were not satisfied; hence the volume now in your hands.

So far we have followed the doings of Dick, Tom, and Sam at dear old Putnam Hall, with many larks and sports; then out upon the broad Atlantic in a daring chase which came pretty close to ending in sad disaster; next into the interior of Africa on a quest of grave importance; and lastly out into the mountainous regions of the wild West, to locate a mining claim belonging to Mr. Anderson Rover.

In the present tale the scene is shifted to the Great Lakes. The three boys go on a pleasure tour and, while on Lake Erie, fall in with an old enemy, who concocts a scheme for kidnapping Dick, who had fallen overboard from his yacht in a storm. This scheme leads to many adventures, the outcome of which will be found in the pages that follow.

In placing this volume in my young readers hands I can but repeat what I have said before: that I am extremely grateful to all for the kind reception given the other Rover Boys stories. I sincerely trust the present tale meets with equal commendation.

Affectionately and sincerely yours,

EDWARD STRATEMEYER.

April 12, 1901

CHAPTER I

A STORM ON LAKE ERIE

"Dick, do you notice how the wind is freshening?"

"Yes, Sam, I've been watching it for ten minutes. I think we are in for a storm."

"Exactly my idea, and I shouldn't be surprised if it proved a heavy one, too. How far are we from shore?"

"Not over three miles, to my reckoning."

"Perhaps we had better turn back," and Sam Rover, the youngest of the three Rover brothers, shook his head doubtfully.

"Oh, I reckon we'll be safe enough," responded Dick Rover, who was several years older. "I know more about sailing a yacht than I did when we followed up the Baxters on the Atlantic Ocean."

"The poor Baxters!" put in Tom Rover, who stood close by, also watching the wind, and the heavy clouds rolling up from the westward. "Who ever supposed that they would be buried alive in that landslide on the mountain in Colorado?"

"It was a terrible fate," came, with a shudder, from Dick Rover. "But, nevertheless, I am glad we are rid of those rascals. They caused father and us trouble enough, goodness knows."

"And they brought trouble enough to Dora Stanhope and her mother, too," observed Sam. "By the way, Dick, weren't Dora and her mother going to take a trip on these lakes this summer?"

"Of course Dora was," put in Tom, with a sly wink. "If she wasn't, what do you suppose would bring Dick here? He got a letter only last week—"

"Oh, stow it, Tom!" cried the elder Rover, his face growing red. "You wanted to take a trip on the Great Lakes as much as anybody—said you wouldn't like anything better, and told all the fellows at Putnam Hall so, too."

"Well, I don't know as I would like anything better," rattled on Tom. "The *Swallow* seems to be a first-class craft, and I've no doubt but what we'll see lots to interest us in this trip from Buffalo to Lake Superior."

"When are the Stanhopes coming out?" asked Sam.

"I can't say, exactly," replied Dick. "I expect another letter from them when we reach Cleveland. In the last letter Dora said her mother was not feeling as well as before."

"A trip on the lakes ought to do her good."

"Wonder if old Josiah Crabtree has been bothering her with his attentions?" came from Tom. "Gosh! how anxious he was to marry her and get hold of the money she is holding in trust for Dora."

"Crabtree's term of imprisonment ran out only last week, Tom. He couldn't annoy her while he was in jail."

"He ought to have been given five years for the way he used them, and us. It's strange what an influence he had over Mrs. Stanhope."

"He's something of a hypnotist, and she seems to be just the right kind of a subject for him. His coming from prison is one reason why Dora wanted to get her mother away. She isn't going to let outsiders know of the trip, so old Crabtree won't know where they are."

"He'll find out, if he can," remarked Sam. "He always was a nosy old chap."

"If he tries any game on, I'll settle him in short order," came from Dick, with determination. "We've put up with enough from him in the past, and I don't intend to give him any leeway in the future."

"Leeway?" burst out Tom. "Not a foot! Not an inch! I haven't forgotten how he treated me when he was a teacher at Putnam Hall. I wonder that Captain Putnam didn't kick him out long before he was made to go."

A sudden rush of wind cut the conversation short at this point, sending the *Swallow* bowling along merrily. The clouds were increasing rapidly, and Dick ordered that all the sails be closely reefed.

"We don't want to lose our mast," he observed.

"We don't want to lose anything," answered Sam. "For my part, I wish we were back in Buffalo harbor."

"Oh! we'll run along all right," came from Tom. "Don't get

scared before you are hurt." He looked at his watch. "Half-past five! I didn't think it was so late."

"It will be dark before long," said Dick. "Perhaps the blow will go down with the setting of the sun."

"We'll never know when the sun sets—excepting by the almanac," murmured Sam. "It's as black as ink already, over to the westward."

To keep up his courage Tom Rover began to whistle, but soon the sound was drowned out by the high piping of the wind, as it tore over the deck and through the rigging of the *Swallow*. They were certainly in for a storm, and a heavy one at that.

It was the middle of July, and the Rover boys had journeyed from Valley Brook, their country home, to Buffalo, a week before, for a six-weeks' outing upon the Great Lakes previous to their returning to Putnam Hall for the fall and winter term. Their thrilling adventures in Colorado, as told in "The Rover Boys Out West," had taxed them severely, and their father, Mr. Anderson Rover, felt that they needed the recreation. At first he had wished them to remain at the farm, and so had their Uncle Randolph Rover and their motherly Aunt Martha, but this had been voted "too slow" by the three brothers, and it was decided that they should go to Buffalo, charter a small yacht, and do as they pleased until the opening of school.

"Only please keep out of danger," had been Mr. Rover's pleading words. "You have been in peril enough." And the boys had promised to do their best, little dreaming of the many adventures and dangers ahead.

The boys knew very little about the lakes, and at the last moment had invited Larry Colby, an old schoolmate, to

Arthur M. Winfield

accompany them on the outing. Larry had spent two summers on Lake Huron and Lake Superior, and knew both bodies of water fairly well. But the lad could not come on at once, and so had sent word that he would join the party at Sandusky, some time later. Larry's father was rich, so the expense of traveling counted for nothing.

With the boys, however, went one individual with whom all our old readers are well acquainted. This was Alexander Pop, the colored man who had once been a waiter at Putnam Hall, and who was now a servant to the Rovers in general and the three boys in particular. The boys had done much in the past for Aleck, as they called him, and Pop was so greatly attached to the youths that he was ready at all times to do anything they desired.

"I dun lub dem Rober boys, aint no ust ter talk," Pop would say. "Dem is de most up-to-date boys in de world, dat's wot, and da did dis yeah niggah a good turn wot he aint forgittin' in a hurry, too." What that good turn was has already been related in full in "The Rover Boys in the Jungle." Pop was now installed on board the *Swallow* as cook and general helper, a position he was well fitted to fill.

The boys had laid out a grand trip, and one which certainly promised a good deal of pleasure. The first stop was to be at Cleveland, and from that city they were to go to Sandusky, and then up the lake and through the Detroit River to Detroit. Here a short stay was to be made, and then the journey was to be resumed through Lake St. Clair and the St. Clair River to Lake Huron. Once on Lake Huron they expected to skirt the eastern coast of Michigan, stopping whenever they pleased, and thus gradually make their way to Whitefish Bay and Lake Superior. What they would do when Lake Superior was reached would depend upon how much time was left for the outing.

The *Swallow* was a well-built, sturdy craft, fifty feet long and correspondingly broad of beam. She had been constructed for a pleasure boat and had all of the latest improvements. She belonged to a rich man of Buffalo, who had known the Rovers for years. The rich man was now traveling in Europe, and had been only too glad to charter the yacht for a period of six weeks. When the Rover boys were through with her she was to be placed in charge of the rich man's boatman, who was to take her back to Buffalo.

The start on Lake Erie had been full of pleasure. The yacht had a good supply of provisions on board, and everybody was in the best of spirits. Aleck Pop had brought along his banjo, and on the first evening out had given them half a dozen plantation songs, for he was a good singer as well as player. On the day following the breeze had died away and they had all gone fishing, with fair success. This was the third day out, and since noon the wind had been blowing at a lively rate, helping them to make good time on their course toward Cleveland. Now the wind was blowing little short of a gale, and the sky was growing blacker each instant.

"We are in for it, beyond a doubt," said Dick, with a serious shake of his head.

Every inch of canvas had been taken in, yet the *Swallow* spun along before the wind rapidly, ever and anon dipping her bow deeply into the white-caps, which now showed themselves upon all sides.

"Here she comes!" burst out Tom suddenly. "Hold hard, everybody!"

And then the storm burst upon them in all of its fury—a storm which lasted all night, and one which the Rover boys never forgot.

CHAPTER II

THE DISAPPEARANCE OF DICK

"Oh, my, but this is a corker!"

It was Tom who uttered the words, half an hour after he had cautioned everybody to hold fast. He was standing at the wheel, helping Dick to make the *Swallow* keep her bow up to the waves, which rolled fiercely on every side of the craft. He cried out at the top of his lungs, yet his elder brother understood him with difficulty.

"I wish we were out of it," returned Dick. "Did Sam go below, as I ordered?"

"Yes."

"What of Aleck?"

"He is in the galley, trying to keep his dishes from being smashed to bits. He is scared, I can tell you, and said he was sure we were going to the bottom."

"If I was sure of the course I would steer for shore, Tom. I'm afraid myself that this is going to be more than we bargained for."

"Pooh, Dick! We've been in as bad a storm before, and you know it."

"But not on Lake Erie. This lake has a reputation for turning out some nasty ones, that do tremendous damage. Light up, will you?—or we may be smashing into some other boat before we know it."

"I will, if you can hold the wheel alone."

"I can get along for a few minutes. But it's enough to pull a fellow's arms out by the sockets," concluded Dick.

With extreme caution, for the deck was as wet and slippery as it was unsteady, Tom made his way to the tiny cabin of the yacht. Here he found Sam lighting the ship's lanterns, four in number.

"I thought you'd be wanting them," said the youngest Rover. "Is it letting up, do you think?"

"No; if anything, it is growing worse."

"Don't you want me to help on deck? I hate to stay down here alone."

"You can do nothing, Sam. Dick and I are tending the wheel, and there is nothing else to be done."

"I might go on the lookout. You can't watch very well from the stern," added the youngest Rover, who did not relish being kept back by his older brothers.

"We can watch good enough. Stay here—it's safer. If the yacht should swing around—Great Scott!"

Tom Rover broke off short, and with good reason. A strange

Arthur M. Winfield

creaking and cracking sound had reached his ears, followed by a bump and a jar which nearly pitched him headlong. Sam was thrown down on his back.

"Something is wrong!" burst out Sam, as soon as he could speak. "We must have struck something."

Tom did not answer, for the reason that he was already on his way to the deck, with a lantern slung in the crook of his right elbow. Sam followed with another lantern, leaving the remaining ones wildly swinging on the hooks in the cabin's ceiling.

"Help! help!"

The cry came from out of the darkness, somewhere in the wake of the *Swallow*; a cry cut partly short by the piping gale. With his heart thumping violently, Tom leaped over the deck toward the wheel.

"Dick! What is the matter?"

"Help!" repeated the voice, but now further off than ever. Then Tom made a discovery which thrilled him with horror.

The position at the wheel was vacant! Dick was gone!

"Dick! Dick! Where are you!" he shouted hoarsely. "Dick!"

"Help!" came more faintly. The cry was repeated several times, but nothing more reached Tom's ears nor the hearing of his younger brother, who was now beside him, his round face as pale as death itself.

"Dick's overboard!" The words came from both, and each looked at the other in consternation.

Both held up their lanterns, the glasses of which were speedily covered with flying spray. The lanterns made a small semicircle of light at the stern, but Dick was beyond that circle and could not be seen.

"Take the wheel—I'll get a life-preserver!" said Tom, and ran for the article he had mentioned.

"Shall I try to turn the yacht around?" questioned his brother, as he, after several unsuccessful attempts, caught the spokes of the wheel, which was flying back and forth with every pitch of the craft.

"No! no! We will be swamped if you do that. Keep her up to the wind."

Regardless of the danger, Tom flew across the deck to where there was a life-preserver, attached to a hundred feet of small, but strong, rope. Once at the stern again, he threw the life-preserver as far out as possible.

"Catch the lifeline!" he shrieked. But if Dick heard he gave no answer.

"Can't we fire a rocket?" said Sam. "We ought to do something," he added, half desperately.

Lashing the end of the lifeline to the stern, Tom ran down into the cabin and brought forth several rockets. With trembling hands he set off first one and then another. The blaze was a short one, yet it revealed to them a large mass of lumber rising and falling on the bosom of the turbulent waters.

"A lumber raft. It is going to pieces in the storm."

"Did you see Dick?"

"I saw two persons on the lumber, but I don't know who they were. They looked more dead than alive."

"Oh, I hope Dick isn't dead!" burst out Sam, and the tears stood in his eyes as he spoke.

"Wot's dat you dun said?" came from out of the darkness.

"Dick's overboard," answered Tom.

"No!" A groan of genuine regret came from Aleck Pop. "How it dun happen?"

"We must have struck a lumber raft and the shock knocked him over," answered Sam. "Oh, Tom, what shall we do?"

"I'll try another rocket, Sam—I don't know of anything else."

It took fully a minute to obtain another rocket, and some red fire as well. The red fire made quite an illumination, in spite of the storm.

"I don't see nuffin," said Pop.

"Nor I," added Tom. "The raft has disappeared."

As the light died out all set up a loud shout. But only the howling wind answered them. And now Sam noticed that the lifeline was drifting idly at the stern, and there was nothing to do but to haul it in again.

The hours which followed were full of agony to Tom and Sam, and the warm-hearted colored man was scarcely less affected.

"What if Dick is drowned?" whispered the youngest Rover.

"Father will never forgive us for coming on this trip."

"Let us hope for the best," was his brother's answer. "Dick has been in a tight fix before. He'll come out all right, if he has any show at all."

"Nobuddy kin lib in sech a storm as dis!" put in Pop. "Why, it's 'most as bad as dat dar hurricane we 'perienced in Africa. Jest see how it's beginnin' to rain."

Pop was right; so far the rain had held off for the most part, but now it came down steadily and soon turned into little short of a deluge. All were speedily soaked to the skin, but this was a discomfort to which, under the circumstances, no one paid attention.

The *Swallow* heaved and pitched, and fearful that Sam would be lost overboard, Tom told him he had better go below again.

"You can do nothing up here," he said. "If anything turns up, I'll call you."

"But you must be careful," pleaded Sam. "If I were you, I'd tie myself to the wheel," and this is what Tom did.

Slowly the night wore away, and with the coming of morning the storm abated somewhat, although the waves still lashed angrily around the *Swallow*. With the first streak of dawn all were on deck, watching anxiously for some sign of the lumber raft or of Dick.

"Nothing in sight!" groaned Sam, and he was right. The raft had disappeared completely, and all around them was a dreary waste of water, with a cloudy sky overhead.

Feeling that he must do something, Aleck Pop prepared a

Arthur M. Winfield

breakfast of broiled fish and hot coffee, but, when summoned to the repast, both of the Rovers shook their heads.

"I couldn't eat a mouthful," sighed Sam. "It would choke me."

"We must find Dick first, Aleck," said Tom. "Go ahead yourself and have breakfast. Don't mind us."

"'Deed, I aint no hungrier dan youse is," replied the colored man soberly. "But youse had bettah drink sum ob dat coffee, or youse might cotch a chill." And he made each sip some of the beverage, bringing it on deck for that purpose.

At half-past seven Tom espied a cloud of smoke on the horizon. "I think it's a lake steamer," he said to his brother, and he proved to be right. It was a freighter known as the *Captain Rallow*, running between Detroit and Buffalo. Soon the steamer came closer and they hailed her.

"Seen anything of a lumber wreck, with some men on it?" questioned Tom eagerly.

"Haven't seen any wreck," was the answer, from the captain of the freighter. "Whose raft was it?"

"I don't know. The raft hit us in the darkness and a young man on our yacht was knocked overboard. We lit some red fire and saw two people on the raft, which seemed to be going to pieces."

This news interested the owner of the freight steamer greatly, since he had a brother who was in the business of rafting lumber, and he asked Tom to give him the particulars of the affair.

"We can't give you any particulars. We were taken

completely by surprise, and it was too dark to see much," said Tom. Nevertheless he and Sam told what they could, to which the freight captain listened with close attention.

"I'll keep my eye open for the raft," said the latter. "And if I see anything of your brother I'll certainly take him on board."

"Where are you bound?"

"I am going to stop at Cleveland first. Then I go straight through to Buffalo."

A few words more passed, and then the captain of the freight steamer gave the signal to go ahead.

The stopping of her engines had caused the steamer to drift quite close to the *Swallow*, and as she swung around those on the yacht caught a good view of the freighter's stern deck.

There were a small number of passengers on board, and as Sam looked them over he gave a sudden start.

"My gracious, can it be possible!" he gasped.

"Can what be possible, Sam?" queried Tom.

"Look! look!"

"At what?"

"At the passengers on the steamer. Am I dreaming, or is that—he is gone!" And Sam's face fell.

"Who are you talking about?"

Arthur M. Winfield

"Arnold Baxter! He was on the steamer, just as sure as I stand here. And we both thought him dead!"

CHAPTER III

ON A LUMBER RAFT

"You think you saw Arnold Baxter?" demanded Tom.

"Yes, I saw Arnold Baxter, just as plain as day."

"Sam, you must be—"

"No, I am not dreaming. It was Arnold Baxter, true enough. As soon as he saw I had spotted him he drew out of sight."

"But we thought he was dead—buried under that landslide out in Colorado."

"We didn't find his body, and he isn't dead. Why, I would never make a mistake in that rascal's face, never," and Sam shook his head to emphasize his words.

"Was Dan with him?"

"I didn't see the son."

"If it was really Arnold Baxter we ought to let the authorities know at once, so that they can arrest him for getting out of prison on that bogus pardon."

Arthur M. Winfield

"Yes, and we ought to let father know, too, for you may be sure Baxter will do all he can to get square with us for keeping the Eclipse mining claim out of his grasp."

"He can't do anything about that claim now. Our claim is established by law, and he is nothing but an escaped jailbird. But I agree he may give us lots of trouble in other directions. I presume he would like to see us all hung for the way we got ahead of him and his tools."

"If the steamer wasn't so far off we might hail her," continued Sam, but this was now out of the question.

Both lads were very much disturbed, and with good reason. Arnold Baxter had been an enemy to Mr. Rover for years, and this meant a good deal when the desperate character of the man was taken into consideration. He was a well-educated fellow, but cruel and unprincipled to the last degree, and one who would hesitate at nothing in order to accomplish his purpose.

"Dat's de wust yet," was Aleck Pop's comment. "I was finkin' dat rascal was plumb dead, suah. And Dan, too! Suah yo' didn't see dat good-fo'-nuffin boy?"

"No, I didn't see Dan."

"He must have been with his father when the landslide occurred," went on Tom. "And if one escaped more than likely the other did, too. My, how I despise that chap! and have, ever since we had our first row with him at Putnam Hall."

"I wonder what brought Arnold Baxter back to this section of the country? I shouldn't think he would dare to come back."

"He always was daring to the last degree in some matters, just as he is cowardly in others. I would give something to know if Dan is with him."

"We might follow up the steamer, if it wasn't for poor Dick."

The boys talked the matter over for some time, and while doing this the sails of the *Swallow* were again hoisted, and they turned the yacht back to the vicinity where Dick had gone overboard.

And while Tom and Sam are looking for their elder brother, let us turn back and learn what really did become of Dick.

He was waiting for Tom to come on deck with the lanterns when, of a sudden, something black and threatening loomed up out of the darkness to the starboard of the *Swallow*.

The mass was the better half of a monstrous lumber raft, which was rapidly going to pieces in the storm.

The raft, or rather what was left of it, hit the *Swallow* a glancing blow, otherwise the sailing craft must have been stove in and sunk.

The shock caught Dick with one hand off the wheel, and, before he could catch hold again, the youth found himself flung heels into the air and over the *Swallow's* stern.

Down and down he went into the lake waters, until he thought he would never come up.

The turn of affairs bewildered him, and he did not come fully to his senses until his head struck one of the timbers of the raft.

He clutched the timber as a drowning man clutches the proverbial straw, and tried to draw himself to the surface of the lake, only to discover, to his horror, that there were timbers to both sides of him, cutting off his further progress upward.

"Must I be drowned like a rat in a trap!" was the agonizing thought which rushed through his brain, and then he pushed along from one timber to another until the last was reached and he came up, almost overcome and panting heavily for breath.

"Help! help!" he cried feebly, and presently heard his brothers answer him. Then the lifeline was thrown, but it fell short and did him no good. By the red fire and the rockets he saw the position of the *Swallow*, and saw his brothers, but was too weak to even signal to Sam and Tom.

It was with an effort that he at last drew himself to the top of some of the lumber. This movement came none too soon, for a moment later one of the outside chains of the raft broke, and fully a third of what was left of the lumber was scattered in all directions.

"Hullo, Bragin! is that you?"

The cry came from out of the darkness and from the other end of the top lumber.

"Are you calling to me?" replied Dick, in as loud a voice as he could muster.

"Is that you, Bragin?" repeated the voice.

"I am not Bragin," answered Dick. "Where are you?"

"Here." And the unknown repeated the cry until Dick

located and joined him. He was a burly lumberman of forty, with a heavy black beard and an equally heavy voice. He gazed at the youth in astonishment.

"Hullo! Where did you come from?" he demanded.

"From the yacht this lumber raft just struck."

"Did the shock knock ye overboard?"

"It did."

"Humph! I thought ye was Bragin."

"I came pretty close to being drowned, for I came up under the lumber."

"Well, we aint out o' the woods yet, young man. Didn't see nuthin o' Bragin, did ye?"

"I've seen nobody but you."

"Then he must be down to the lake bottom by this time."

"He was on the raft with you?"

"Yes. He and I left the tug to see to the chains when the storm came up."

"Where is the tug?"

"The raft broke away from her at the fust blow. A fool of a greenhorn was a-managin' of the thing, an' this is the result. Come here—it's safer."

Dick was perfectly willing to crawl closer to the burly lumberman, who was a good fellow, as could be seen by

Arthur M. Winfield

a glance.

"We'll be all right, if this section o' the lumber keeps together," went on the lumberman. "There are four chains here, so it ought to hold."

Once safe, for the time being, Dick began to wonder about the fate of the *Swallow*.

"Did the yacht go down?" he asked anxiously.

"I reckon not, young man. They burned red fire, you know. They wouldn't do that if there was much trouble aboard."

"That is true." Dick was silent for a moment. "I wish I could get back to her."

"Be thankful that ye aint at the bottom o' the lake. If we kin outride this storm we'll be safe enough, for the tug will be lookin' for the raft when it gits light."

Slowly the hours wore away, and in the meanwhile Dick learned that the lumberman's name was Luke Peterson and that he was from the timberlands of Michigan.

"I used to be in the United States service on the lakes, hunting down smugglers between here and Canada," said Peterson. "But that was years ago."

"Do they do much smuggling?" asked Dick.

"More than most folks think," was the decided answer.

The lumberman listened to Dick's tale with interest. Of course the story had to be short, and was frequently interrupted, as high waves would come along and almost sweep them into the lake. Both lay flat, clutching at the lumber and at the huge chains which held it, and which had thus far refused to part, although the strain upon them were tremendous.

It was about two o'clock in the morning when the storm, according to Dick's calculation, reached its height. The waves literally drove over the raft from end to end, and it was all both he and Luke Peterson could do to keep on the timbers.

"Hold on tight, young man, if ye value your life!" roared the lumberman. "An' if the raft parts, stick to the fust timber ye lay hands on."

Peterson had scarcely spoken when the raft went up to the top of a mighty wave and then came down with a dull boom in the hollow below. The shock was terrific, and it was followed by loud reports as the chains they had been depending upon snapped, one after another. Immediately the lumber loosened up and began to drift apart.

"Take care a' yerself!" shouted the lumberman, and hung fast to an extra long and heavy log. Dick heard him, but could not answer for fear of getting his mouth full of water. The youth turned over and over, clutched at one log and missed it, missed a second and a third, and then touched a fourth, and clung with a deathlike grip that nothing could loosen.

It was a soul-trying time, and one which poor Dick never forgot. The storm roared all around him, mingled with the thumping and bumping, grinding and crashing, of the sticks of timber. Once his left leg was caught between two sticks, and for the instant he was afraid the limb would be crushed. But then the pressure lessened and he drew the foot up in a hurry. The water washed into his face and over him, and he caught his breath with difficulty. Each instant looked as if it might be his last.

Arthur M. Winfield

CHAPTER IV

IN THE HANDS OF THE ENEMY

Daylight found poor Dick all but exhausted. He still held to the stick of lumber, but his hands were numb and without feeling, and his lower limbs were in the same condition.

"I can't stand this much longer," was his dismal thought. "I've got to let go soon."

He looked around him anxiously. All that met his eyes was the broad expanse of water, with here and there a solitary stick of lumber. He gazed about for Luke Peterson, but the lumberman was not in sight.

"He must have been drowned," he thought. "Heaven help me, or I'll go, too!"

Gradually the sky cleared of the clouds, and the hot July sun began to pour down with a glare on the water that was well-nigh blinding. As the waves went down he changed his position on the log, and this gave him temporary relief. Soon the sun made his head ache, and he began to see strange visions. Presently he put out his hand, thinking that Tom was before him, and then went with a splash into the lake.

Almost unconscious of what he was doing, he caught the log again. But he was now too weak to pull himself up. "It's the end," he thought bitterly. Then a cry came to him, a cry that seemed half real, half imaginary.

"Hullo, Rover! Is that you?"

It was Peterson who was calling. The lumberman had drifted up on another log, and as the two sticks bumped together he caught hold of the youth and assisted him to his former resting place.

"I—I can't hold on any—any longer!" gasped Dick.

"Try, lad, try! Some kind of a boat is bound to appear, sooner or later."

"I—I am nu—numb all over."

"I suppose that's true—I'm numb myself. But don't ye give up."

Encouraged somewhat by Peterson's words Dick continued to hold on, and a few minutes later the lumberman gave a cheering cry:

"A steamer! Saved at last!"

The lumberman was right; the freighter Tom and Sam had hailed was approaching, the castaways having been discovered by the aid of a marine glass.

"A man and a boy," observed Captain Jasper to his mate.

"The boy looks pretty well done for," returned the mate. "He must be the one that was thrown off the yacht."

Arthur M. Winfield

"More than likely."

As speedily as possible the freight steamer drew closer, and a line was thrown to Peterson.

He turned to give one end to Dick, and then made the discovery that the latter had fainted from exhaustion.

"Poor fellow!" he muttered, and caught the youth just as he was sliding into the lake.

It was no easy task to get Dick on board of the freight steamer. But it was accomplished at last, and, still unconscious, he was carried to a stateroom and made as comfortable as possible.

Peterson was but little the worse for the adventure, and his chief anxiety was for his friend Bragin, of whom, so far, nothing had been heard.

The coming of Dick on board of the *Captain Rollow* was viewed with much astonishment by two of the passengers on the freighter.

These two persons were Arnold Baxter and his son Dan.

The two had quite recovered from the injuries received in the landslide in Colorado, and it may be as well to state right here that they were bound East in order to carry out a new plot which the elder Baxter had hatched up against the Rovers.

What that plot was will be disclosed as our story proceeds.

"Father, it is Dick Rover," cried Dan Baxter, after having seen the unconscious one brought on board.

"Hush, Dan! I know it," whispered Arnold Baxter.

"It's a pity he wasn't drowned in the lake."

"I agree with you. But he isn't dead, and we'll have to keep out of sight for the rest of the trip."

"Humph! I am not afraid of him!" said the bully, for, as old readers know, Dan had never been anything else.

"That may be, but if he sees us he may—ahem—make much trouble for me."

"On account of our doings in Colorado? What can he prove? Nothing."

"Perhaps he can. Besides, Dan, you must remember that the officers of New York State are still after me."

"Yes, I haven't forgotten that."

"I wish now that I had put on that false wig and beard before we left Detroit," went on Arnold Baxter. "But I hated to put them on before it was absolutely necessary—the weather is so warm."

"Can you put them on now?"

"Hardly, since all on board know my real looks. I will have to keep out of Rover's sight."

"I would like to know what he is doing out here."

"On a pleasure trip, most likely."

The talk went on for some time, and then Dan approached one of the mates of the freighter, who had just come from

Arthur M. Winfield

the stateroom to which Dick had been taken.

"How is that young fellow getting on?" he asked carelessly.

"He's in bad shape," was the answer.

"Do you think he'll die?"

"Hardly, but he is very weak and completely out of his mind. The hot sun, coming after the storm, must have affected his brain."

"Out of his mind? Doesn't he recognize anybody?"

"No, he talks nothing but lumber, and cries out to be pulled from the water. Poor boy! it's too bad, isn't it?"

"It is too bad," said Dan Baxter hypocritically. "Do you know his name?"

"No, but he's a brother to those boys who hailed us from the yacht a couple of hours ago. A lumber raft struck the yacht and the boy was knocked overboard and managed to cling to some timber."

"Is the man who was saved his friend?"

"No, he was on the raft and the two are strangers;" and with this remark the mate of the freight steamer passed on.

Without delay Dan told his father of what he had heard. Arnold Baxter was much pleased.

"If he remains out of his mind we'll be safe enough," he said. "I presume they'll put him off at Cleveland and send him to the hospital."

"I wonder where that yacht is?"

"Oh, we have left her miles behind."

"And how soon will we reach Cleveland?"

"Inside of half an hour, so I heard one of the deck hands say."

No more was said for the time being, but both father and son set to thinking deeply, and their thoughts ran very much in the same channel.

Just as the freight steamer was about to make the landing at Cleveland, Arnold Baxter touched his son on the arm.

"If they take Dick Rover ashore, let us go ashore too," he whispered.

"I was thinking of that, dad," was Dan's answer. "Was you thinking, too, of getting him in our power?"

"Yes."

"I don't see why we can't do it—if he is still unconscious."

"It won't hurt to try. But we will have to work quick, for more than likely his brothers will follow us to this city," went on Arnold Baxter.

The steamer had but little freight for Cleveland, so the stop was only a short one.

When poor Dick was brought up on a cot, still unconscious, Arnold Baxter stepped forward.

"I have determined to stop off at Cleveland," he said to

Arthur M. Winfield

Captain Jasper. "If there is anything I can do for this poor fellow, I will do it willingly."

"Why, I thought you were going through to Buffalo," returned the captain in surprise.

"I was going through, but I've just remembered some business that must be attended to. I'll take the train for Buffalo to-morrow. If you want me to see to it that this poor fellow is placed in the hospital, I'll do it."

The offer appeared a good one, and relieved Captain Jasper's mind greatly.

"You are kind, sir," he said. "It isn't everyone who would put himself to so much trouble."

"I was wrecked myself once," smiled Arnold Baxter. "And I know how miserable I felt when nobody gave me a hand."

"I suppose the authorities will take him until his brothers come in on that yacht."

"There is no need to send him to a public institution. I will see to it that he gets to a first-class hotel," went on Arnold Baxter smoothly.

There was a little more talk, and then Dick was carried ashore and a coach was called.

By this time the freight steamer was ready to leave, and a minute later she proceeded on her way.

Arnold Baxter and Dan looked around and saw only a few people at hand. In the crowd was Luke Peterson, who now came forward.

"Want any help?" asked the lumberman respectfully.

"You might keep an eye open for that yacht," replied Arnold Baxter.

"All right, sir. Where are you going to take young Rover?"

"To the Commercial Hotel. I am well known there, and can easily get him a good room and the necessary medical attention."

"Then, if I see anything of the yacht, I'll send his brothers up to the hotel after him."

"That's it," returned Arnold Baxter. He turned to the driver of the coach. "To the Commercial Hotel," he went on, in a loud voice. "And drive as easy as you can."

Dan was already in the coach, supporting poor Dick in his arms. Arnold Baxter leaped in and banged the door shut. Soon the coach was moving away from the water front and in the direction of the hotel which had been mentioned.

"Of course you are not going to the Commercial Hotel," observed Dan, as soon as he felt safe to speak.

"Leave it all to me, my son," was Arnold Baxter's reply. "We got him away nicely, didn't we?"

"Yes, but—"

"Never mind the future, Dan. How is he?"

"Dead as a stone, so far as knowing anything is concerned."

"I trust he remains so, for a while at least."

Arthur M. Winfield

The coach rattled on, and presently came to a halt in front of the hotel which had been mentioned.

"Wait here until I get back," said Arnold Baxter to his son and to the coach driver, and then hurried inside of the building.

Instead of asking for a room he spent a few minutes in looking over a business directory.

"It's too bad, but they haven't a single room vacant," he said, on coming back to the coach. "I've a good mind to take him to some private hospital, after all. Do you know where Dr. Karley's place is?" he went on, turning to the coach driver.

"Yes."

"Then drive us to that place."

Again the coach went on. Dr. Karley's Private Sanitarium was on the outskirts of Cleveland, and it took half an hour to reach it. It was an old-fashioned building surrounded by a high board fence. Entering the grounds, Arnold Baxter ascended the piazza and rang the bell.

A negro answered the summons, and ushered him into a dingy parlor. Soon Dr. Karley, a dried-up, bald-headed, old man appeared.

"And what can I do for you, sir?" he asked, in a squeaky voice.

"Just the man I wanted to meet," thought Arnold Baxter.

He was a good reader of character, and saw that Dr. Karley would do almost anything for money.

The doctor's sanitarium was of a "shady" character. Among the inmates were two old men, put there by their relatives merely to get them out of the way, and an old lady who was said to be crazy by those who wished to get possession of her money.

"I have a peculiar case on hand, doctor," said Arnold Baxter, after introducing himself as Mr. Arnold. "A young friend of mine has been almost drowned in the lake. I would like you to take charge of him for a day or two."

"Well, I—er—"

"I will pay you well for your services," went on Arnold Baxter.

"You have him with you?"

"Yes, in a coach outside. He was found drifting on a log and almost out of his head on account of exposure to the water and the hot sun. I think a few days of rest and medical attention will bring him around all right."

The little old doctor bobbed his head. "I will go out and see him," he said.

Quarter of an hour later found Dick in an upper room of the sanitarium, lying on a comfortable bed, and with Dr. Karley caring for him.

In the meantime Arnold Baxter had gone out and paid the coach driver.

"Do you generally stand down by the docks?" he asked.

"No, sir; my stand is uptown," was the reply. "I had just brought down a passenger when you hailed me. But I can go down for you, if you wish."

"It will not be necessary. The doctor has a carriage, and I will hire that later on, when I see how the patient is making out"

"All right, sir; then I'm off."

As the coach passed out of sight Arnold Baxter chuckled to himself.

"I reckon that was well done," he muttered. "I don't believe the Rovers will find their brother very soon, if they ever find him!"

CHAPTER V

THE SAILING OF THE "PEACOCK"

"Oh, my, what a bad dream I have had!"

Such were the words which Dick uttered to himself when he came once again to the full possession of his senses.

He gazed around him curiously. He was in a plainly furnished room, lying on the top of a bed covered with a rubber blanket, so that his wet clothing might not soil the linen beneath. His coat and shoes had been removed, likewise his collar and tie, but that was all.

The shades of the two windows of the apartment were tightly drawn and a lamp on the table lit up the room but dimly, for it was now night. No one was present but the sufferer.

"Well, one thing is certain, I didn't drown, after all," he went on. Then he tried to sit up, but fell back exhausted.

He wondered where he was, and if Tom and Sam were near, and while he was wondering he fell into a light sleep which did a great deal toward restoring him to himself.

When Dick awoke he found Dr. Karley at hand, ready to

give him some nourishing food. The doctor had just come from a long talk with Arnold Baxter, and it may as well be stated that the two men understood each other pretty thoroughly.

"Where am I?" he asked, in a fairly strong voice.

"Safe," said the old doctor soothingly. "Here, take this. It will do you a whole lot of good."

"Are my brothers around?"

"We'll talk later, after you are stronger."

The old doctor would say no more. Dick took the medicine offered, and did really feel stronger. Then a light breakfast was brought in, of which he partook readily. The food gone, the doctor disappeared, locking the door after him, but so softly that Dick was not aware of the fact until some time later.

While Dick was trying to get back his strength the Baxters were not idle.

Arnold Baxter had on his person all the money he possessed, a little over three thousand dollars. This had been saved from the wreck of his expedition to the West, and he was now resolved to spend every dollar of it, if necessary, in bringing the Rovers to terms, as he put it.

"I was going to New York State to get the youngest Rover boy in my power," he said to Dan, "but fate has thrown Dick in our path, and so we will take him instead. Once he is absolutely in our power, I am sure I can bring Anderson Rover to terms and make him turn the entire right to that Eclipse mine over to my representatives."

"It's a ticklish job," replied the son. "What of this doctor here? Won't he suspect anything?"

"I reckon the doctor is no better than he ought to be, Dan. I think I see my way clear to doing as I please with him. A couple of hundred dollars will go a long way with fellows of his stripe."

A conversation lasting half an hour followed, and Dan promised to keep close watch while his father went away to the docks.

Arnold Baxter was absent the best part of the morning, but came home with a face which showed he was well satisfied with what he had accomplished.

"I fell in luck," he explained. "Ran across a man I used to know years ago—Gus Langless—a sly old dog, up for anything with money in it. Langless owns a small schooner, the *Peacock*, and be says I can have her for a month, with the services of himself and his crew, for one thousand dollars—and nothing said about the job."

"Did you accept, dad?"

"Certainly—it was just what I wanted. Langless is all right, and I told him I would double his money if he would stick by me to the finish, and he swore that he would."

"And what is the next move?"

"We'll take Rover on board to-night, and then set sail direct for Detroit and Lake Huron. Langless knows an island in Lake Huron which will give us just the hiding place we want."

"And after that?"

"I'll send a letter to Anderson Rover which will sicken him to the heart and make him do just as I demand. He thinks the world of his oldest son."

"Good for you, dad! You've got a long head on your shoulders. And when are you going to let Dick Rover know he is in our power?"

"Not until we have him on the *Peacock*, if I can prevent it. If he knew here, he might kick up a big row."

"Pooh! we could easily shut him up!" sniffed Dan.

Now Dick was in their custody he was impatient to browbeat the youth and taunt him with his helplessness. But Arnold Baxter would not listen to it, so the graceless son had to bide his time.

The afternoon was an anxious one for both of the Baxters, who were afraid that the Rovers would find their way to Dr. Karley's place and thwart their carefully arranged plan. But no one put in an appearance, and by nightfall everything was in readiness for the departure. The doctor had loaned his private turnout, and for a "consideration," otherwise a bribe, had dosed poor Dick into semi-unconsciousness, and had promised to say to all comers that the young man had got well and gone off in the company of two of his friends, a Mr. Arnold and a Mr. Daniels.

When it came to transferring Dick to the carriage, Arnold Baxter put on the false wig and beard which he had been carrying in his valise, thus transforming his appearance greatly. Dan kept out of sight on the seat of the carriage, so that Dick saw only his back in the gloom of the night. The son drove while Arnold Baxter held Dick.

It was no easy matter to find the location of the *Peacock*, and equally difficult to get Dick on board without observation. But Captain Langless had wisely sent his men to a neighboring saloon, so the coast was tolerably clear. Once Dick was in the cabin, Arnold Baxter left him in Dan's charge and hurried back to the sanitarium with the turnout. In the meantime Captain Langless summoned his sailors and told them they would sail at early dawn—half-past four.

Locking the door of the cabin and putting the key in his pocket, Dan Baxter turned up the light and then looked at Dick, who lay half propped up in a chair.

"I guess I'll wake him up," he muttered, and going over to the helpless youth he pulled his nose vigorously.

"Oh!" groaned Dick, and opened his eyes dreamily. Then he caught sight of Dan and stared as if he had seen a ghost.

"Dan Baxter!" he said slowly. "Can it be possible?"

"Yes, it's me," replied the bully, with small regard for grammar. "Do you know that you are in my power, Dick Rover?"

"I—I—thought you were dead," and Dick closed his eyes again, for it was next to impossible for him to arouse himself.

"I'm a long way from being dead," laughed Dan harshly. "I reckon you'll die before I do."

Dick pulled himself together with a great effort.

"Then the landslide didn't catch you?" he questioned.

"Yes, it did, but it didn't kill me, nor my father neither. We are both here, and you are absolutely in our power."

"Is this the steamer that took me on board?"

"No, this is a boat that is under my father's command."

"I don't understand it at all."

"Reckon you will understand before we are done with you. You thought you could crow over us, but the crowing will be on the other side of the fence now."

"What are you going to do with me?"

"You'll find out soon enough."

"Where are my brothers?"

"I don't know—and I don't care."

"Well, I am glad they are not in your power," returned Dick, with something of a sigh of relief.

"One of you is enough," growled Dan.

"And you won't tell me what boat this is?"

"It is one under the command of my father."

"Are we sailing?"

"Not yet, but we will be in a few minutes."

With an effort Dick arose to his feet. But he was dizzy from the effects of the dose administered by the doctor, and immediately sank back again. Baxter gave a brutal laugh.

"Now you see how it is," he observed. "You are absolutely in our power. How do you like the situation?"

"How should I like it? A lamb among wolves would be as safe, to my way of thinking."

"I don't know but what you are right. We intend to make a big thing out of you, Dick Rover."

"How?"

"I told you before you'd find out soon enough."

"I presume you'll try to make my father ransom me, or something like that."

"We'll about make him give up that mining claim."

"You were going to make him give that up before."

"Well, we won't trip up this time. Our plans are carefully laid."

"You were always good at bragging, Dan Baxter."

"Don't insult me, Dick Rover."

"I am telling the plain truth."

With a sudden darkening of his face Dan Baxter strode forward.

"Dick Rover, I hate you, always have hated you, and always will hate you. Take that for your impudence."

He struck out and slapped the helpless boy heavily upon the cheek. Then, as Dick sank back in the chair, he turned and left the cabin, closing and locking the door after him.

At half-past four in the morning the *Peacock* got under way, and in less than an hour was far out upon the broad waters of Lake Erie.

CHAPTER VI

HUNTING FOR DICK

"Dick must be drowned."

It was Tom who spoke, addressing Sam and Aleck Pop.

For hours they had searched among the floating lumber for some sign of the missing one, and the only thing that had been found was Dick's cap, caught in a crack of one of the timbers.

"It's awful!" murmured Sam. His face was white and he was ready to cry, for Dick was very dear to him.

"Perhaps dat steamboat dun pick him up," suggested Pop. He wanted to say something comforting.

"I pray to Heaven she did," murmured Tom. "I suppose the best thing we can do now is to steer for Cleveland."

"Yes, that's the only hope left," answered Sam. "If he was floating around here we would surely have spotted him before this with the glass."

The course was changed, and toward nightfall they came in sight of Cleveland, and learned where they could tie up, at a

Arthur M. Winfield

spot close to where the steamer had made her landing.

Their first inquiries were at this point, and from a long-shoreman they quickly learned that two persons had been picked up by the steamer, a big man and a young fellow.

"It must be Dick!" cried Sam.

"Where did they take the young fellow?" questioned Tom.

"A man and a big boy came from the steamer and took charge of him," answered the longshoreman.

"Don't you know where they went?"

"No; most likely to the hospital. The young fellow was in pretty bad shape. They got in a coach."

"Did the other man who was saved go along?"

"No; he's all right, and is around here looking for you folks—so he told me. He—here he comes now."

The longshoreman pointed to Luke Peterson, who had just appeared at the upper end of the dock. Both Sam and Tom ran to meet him.

"So you are Dick Rover's brothers," said Peterson, as he shook hands. "Glad to know you. Yes, your brother is all right, although mighty tucked out by the exposure. He fell in with a couple o' friends on the steamer, and they took him up to the Commercial Hotel."

As Peterson was curious to know how Dick was faring, he agreed to accompany Sam and Tom to the hotel, and all three boarded a handy street car for that purpose.

"I wish to see my brother, Dick Rover," said Tom to the clerk at the desk.

"Not stopping here, sir," was the reply, after the clerk had consulted the register.

"I mean the young man who was hauled out of the lake and was brought here feeling rather sick."

The clerk shook his head. "No such person here."

Sam and Tom stared in astonishment, and then turned to the lumberman.

"The friends who were with him said they were going to bring him here," said Luke Peterson. "And I promised to send you after 'em as soon as I spotted ye."

"I don't understand—" began Tom, and then turned swiftly to Sam. "Can this be some of Arnold Baxter's work?"

"It may be. Mr. Peterson, how did the man who was with my brother look?"

As well as he could Luke Peterson described Arnold Baxter, and also Dan. Tom gave a low whistle.

"I'll wager poor Dick has fallen into the hands of the enemy," he cried.

"What enemy?" questioned the lumberman.

In as few words as possible Tom and Sam explained the situation, concluding by saying they had discovered Arnold Baxter on the steamer. The story made Luke Peterson look very grave.

"Reckon we let your brother git into the wrong hands," he observed.

"The question is, where did they take Dick?"

"That's so, where?"

"Evidently they didn't come here at all."

"Perhaps, if I could find that coach driver, I might learn somethin'."

"That's so—let us find him by all means."

But to find the driver was not easy, and by midnight the search was abandoned. Much dejected, Sam and Tom returned to the *Swallow*, and Luke Peterson accompanied them. Peterson was also downhearted, having heard nothing of the tug which had been towing the lumber raft or of his friend Bragin.

"I'll notify the police in the morning," said Tom, and did so. He also sent a telegram to his father, telling of what had happened. The police took up the case readily, but brought nothing new to light.

"I'm going to interview every cabby in town," said Tom, and proceeded to do so, accompanied by Luke Peterson and Sam.

At five o'clock in the afternoon they found the coach driver who had taken Dick from the dock.

"The man said they had no rooms vacant at the Commercial Hotel," said the coach driver. "So he had me drive the party to Dr. Karley's Private Sanitarium."

"Where is that?"

"On the outskirts, about a mile and a half from here."

"Can you take us there now?"

"Sorry, but I've got a job in quarter of an hour."

"We'll pay you double fare," put in Sam. "Get somebody else to take that other job."

To this the coach driver readily agreed, but to make the arrangement took time, and it was six o'clock before they were on the way to Dr. Karley's place.

When they reached the sanitarium they found the building dark, with the shutters on the ground floor tightly closed. Dr. Karley answered Tom's summons in person.

"Yes, the parties were here," he said smoothly. "But I could not accommodate them, and so they went elsewhere."

"Elsewhere?" echoed Tom.

"Exactly, sir."

"But our coach driver says they got off here. He was the one who brought them."

At this announcement the face of the physician changed color for an instant. But he quickly recovered himself.

"Well—er—they did get off here, as the sick young man wished to rest. When I said I couldn't accommodate them the older man went off and got another coach, and all three went off in that."

"To where?"

"I do not know, although I recommended the general hospital to them."

"They did not go to any of the city institutions."

"Then perhaps they went to a hotel."

"We have inquired at every hotel in town."

The little old doctor shrugged his bony shoulders. "I am sorry, but I can give you no further information."

"How was the sick young man when he was here?"

"He didn't appear to be very sick. Had he been bad I would have certainly done more for him."

"And you haven't the least idea where they went to?"

"I have not."

"It's mighty strange," was Tom's blunt comment. "Do you know who the sick young man was?"

"I haven't the slightest idea. I never ask questions unless they are necessary."

"He was my brother, and those fellows who had him in charge are his enemies and up to no good."

"Indeed!" And Dr. Karley elevated his shaggy eyebrows in well-assumed surprise.

"I am bound to find my brother, and if you know anything more you had better tell me," went on Tom bluntly.

The random shaft struck home, and the old doctor started back in dismay.

"Why—er—surely you do not—er—suspect me of—ahem —of anything wrong?" he stammered.

"I want to get at the truth. Which way did they go when they drove off?"

"Directly for town."

"And when was this?"

"Inside of half an hour after they got here."

"Did they give any names?"

"No. It was not necessary, since I could not take them in."

"Your place doesn't seem to be very crowded."

At this the physician glared angrily at Tom.

"Boy, it seems to me that you are growing impudent!" he cried. "I am not accustomed to being addressed in this fashion. I think I had better bid you good-night."

The two were standing in the hallway, and now the doctor opened the door to signify that the interview was over.

"All right, I'll go," muttered Tom. "But I am going to get to the bottom of this affair, don't you forget that." And then he hurried out and rejoined Sam and Peterson at the coach.

"He may be telling the truth," said the coach driver, on hearing what Tom had to say. "But, all the same, I was driving around these streets for a good hour after I left here, and I saw no other rig with those men and your brother in it."

"I am inclined to think the doctor is humbugging us," answered Tom. "But the thing is to prove it."

"Perhaps you had better watch the place for a while," suggested the lumberman.

"Do you know anything of this doctor—what sort of a reputation he has?" asked Sam of the driver.

"His reputation is none of the best," was the answer. "He has been in court twice because of the people he treats."

"Then he wouldn't be above helping Arnold Baxter—if he was paid for it," said Tom.

All entered the coach and drove off around the nearest corner.

Then Tom and Sam got out and walked away, intending to come up at the rear of the sanitarium.

Presently a carriage appeared in view, driven by a man who, in the gloom, appeared strangely familiar, despite his false beard.

"Arnold Baxter!" cried Sam. "Hi, there, whoa!"

He ran toward the carriage and caught the horse by the bridle. Tom followed, and the man, who was just returning from taking Dick to the *Peacock*, was brought to bay.

CHAPTER VII

THE ESCAPE OF ARNOLD BAXTER

"Arnold Baxter, where is my brother Dick?" demanded Tom, as he reached the carriage and caught the evildoer by the arm.

To say that Arnold Baxter was astonished would be to put it altogether too mildly. He was completely dumfounded.

"You!" he said slowly, hardly knowing how to speak after he had caught his breath.

"Yes, you rascal. Where is Dick."

"Dick?"

"Yes, Dick."

"I know nothing of your brother. This is a—a complete surprise. I didn't know you were in Cleveland."

"Perhaps not. But let me tell you that we know your game, and we are going to hand you over to the law."

"Never!" Arnold Baxter fairly hissed out the words. "Let go of that horse"—the latter words to Sam.

Arthur M. Winfield

"Don't you do it!" cried Tom, and then he caught Arnold Baxter by the leg. "Come out of the carriage."

A fierce struggle ensued, and, afraid that Tom would get the worst of it, Sam set up a loud shout for help.

"You whelp! I'll fix you!" ejaculated Arnold Baxter, and catching up the whip, he struck at Tom with the butt end. He caught the youth directly over the head, and Tom went down as if shot.

"Let Tom alone," screamed Sam. "Help! help!"

"Who is it?" came from a distance, and Luke Peterson hove into sight. "Hullo! the man we are after."

He made a dive for Arnold Baxter, but the latter was too quick for him, and leaped from the opposite side of the carriage to the ground. The horse now became frightened and set off on a run, directly for a lane behind Dr. Karley's institution.

"Tom, are you badly hurt?" questioned Sam, but, even as he spoke, Tom tried to stagger to his feet. Seeing this, Sam began a chase after Baxter, with the lumberman beside him.

Arnold Baxter was fleet of foot, and realizing what capture meant—a return to prison with his sentence to be served once more from the beginning—he ran as never before, straight for the dock where the *Peacock* lay.

His first thought was to board the schooner and set sail out into the lake, but a second thought convinced him that this would be unwise.

"They will follow me on a tug or steamer, and the jig will be up in no time," he said to himself "I must find some hiding place."

Many of the docks were inclosed by high board fences, and coming to one of these, he leaped over and made his way to a huge pile of merchandise. Here he crouched down and kept as quiet as a mouse.

Sam and Peterson, followed by Tom, traced him to the fence, but once on the opposite side, lost all track of the rascal.

"He's gone," said Tom, after running hither and thither on the dock. "He has given us the slip nicely."

"He can't be far off," returned Sam. "I believe he was bound for that doctor's sanitarium when we spotted him."

"So do I, and I wouldn't wonder if poor Dick is at the place, a prisoner."

The matter was talked over for several minutes, and the two brothers decided to return to Dr. Karley's sanitarium. The lumberman said he would remain around the docks on the lookout for Arnold Baxter.

"If you catch him I'll give you fifty dollars," said Tom. "My father, I know, will pay the amount willingly."

"I'll do my best," answered Peterson. He was by no means rich and glad enough of a chance to make such a sum. Besides this, the ways of the Rover boys appeared to please him.

When Sam and Tom returned to the doctor's place they found the coach driver still at hand, he having caught Arnold Baxter's horse at the entrance to the lane.

Arthur M. Winfield

"Take him to the stable and ask the doctor if the rig is his," said Tom, and the coach driver agreed. He was gone the best part of quarter of an hour.

"The doctor says it is his horse and carriage, but he also says he didn't know the turnout was out," he announced, with a grin. "He's an oily one, he is!"

"Right you are, but he can't stuff us with his fairy tales," replied Tom. "Do you suppose there is a policeman handy?"

"There is probably one somewhere around."

"I wish you would hunt him up and bring him here."

"What are you going to do?"

"Dare the lion in his den; eh, Sam?"

"Right, Tom! That doctor must know a good deal more than he is wiling to tell."

The coach driver went off, and walking around to the front of the sanitarium the boys rang the bell sharply.

There was no answer to the summons, and then Tom gave the bell knob a jerk which nearly broke it off. A second-story window was thrown open with a bang.

"I want you boys to go away!" came in angry tones.

"And I want you to come down and let us in," retorted Tom.

"I won't let you in. I've told you all I know, and that is the end of it."

"It's not the end of it, Dr. Karley. We want to know how you came to let Arnold Baxter have your horse and carriage."

"I didn't know the horse and carriage were out of the stable. The man must have taken them on the sly."

"It's not likely. Open the door and let us in—it will be best for you."

"Ha, you threaten me!"

"I've done more than that-I've sent for a policeman."

At this announcement the old doctor grated his teeth savagely. He was much disturbed and knew not how to proceed.

"I was a fool to go into this thing," he muttered. "It may lead to all sorts of trouble. I must get myself clear somehow."

"Are you going to let us in?" went on Tom.

"Yes, I will let you in. But allow me to state that you are acting very foolishly," answered the doctor, and dropped the window. A few minutes later he appeared at the door, which he opened very gingerly.

"You can come into the parlor," he said stiffly.

"We'll remain right here," answered Tom, afraid of some sort of a trap.

"Well, what do you want?"

"I want to know where that young man, my brother, is."

Arthur M. Winfield

"The man who was with him said he was his nephew."

"It was a falsehood. Now where is my brother?"

"Honestly, I have not the slightest idea."

"What was that man doing with your carriage?"

"I repeat, young man, I did not know he had the carriage." The old doctor drew a long breath, wondering how soon an officer of the law would appear. "Of course if anything is wrong I am perfectly willing to do all I can to set it right. My institution is above reproach, and I wish to keep it so."

"Are you willing to let me look through your place?"

"So you think your brother is here?"

"I do."

"You are very forward. Still, to convince you that you are mistaken, you are at liberty to go through my place from top to bottom. But you must not disturb any of the patients."

"All right; let us go through. Sam, you remain here, on the watch for that policeman."

With bad grace Dr. Karley led the way and took Tom through the sanitarium from top to bottom, even allowing him to peep into the rooms occupied by the "boarders," as the medical man called them. Of course there was no trace of Dick.

"Now I trust you are satisfied," said the doctor, when they were again at the front door.

"I am not satisfied about that carriage affair," returned Tom, as bluntly as ever.

"Well, I have told you the truth."

At this moment the coach driver came in sight, accompanied by a policeman.

"What's the trouble?" demanded the officer of the law.

Tom and Sam told their tale, and then the doctor had his say, and the driver related what he knew.

"Certainly a queer mix-up," remarked the policeman. He turned to the Rovers. "What do you want to do?"

"I want to find my brother, who has disappeared," said Tom.

"You say you have searched through here?"

"I have—after a fashion."

"You can go through, if you wish," said the doctor to the officer.

"I reckon my brother is gone," went on Tom. "But this doctor helped the rascals who spirited him away."

"I did absolutely nothing," cried Dr. Karley. "I am willing to aid you all I can. But I am innocent. I received no pay for giving the unfortunate young man some medicine to strengthen him, and my horse and carriage were taken without my knowledge."

A long and bitter war of words followed, but in the end the doctor was left to himself.

"We'll make no charge against him yet," said Tom to the policeman. "But I wish you would keep an eye on the institution—in case that rascal puts in an appearance again."

"I will," returned the officer.

A little while later Sam and Tom set out to rejoin Luke Peterson. When they gained the dock they saw nobody.

"He ought to be somewhere about," said the younger Rover.

They tramped about from place to place for fully an hour.

Presently they came close to where the *Swallow* lay. Had they but known it, the *Peacock*, with poor Dick on board, lay but three blocks further away.

"My gracious!" cried Sam suddenly.

He had seen a form stretched motionless across some lumber lying near.

The form was that of Luke Peterson, and his cheek and temple were covered with blood.

CHAPTER VIII

ON THE LAKE AGAIN

"Peterson!" cried Tom, in dismay.

"Can he be dead?" came from Sam. Then he bent over the lumberman. "No, he still lives. But he has been treated most shamefully."

"This must be some more of Arnold Baxter's work"

"Or else the work of some footpad."

Both boys knelt over the prostrate form of the lumberman and did what they could to restore him to his senses.

In this they were partly successful.

"Don't hit me again! Please don't hit me!" the man moaned, over and over again.

"You're safe," said Tom. But Peterson paid no attention, and only begged them not to hit him.

"Let us carry him to the *Swallow*," suggested Sam, and between them they did so.

Arthur M. Winfield

"Wot's dis?" asked Aleck Pop, in astonishment.

"He is our friend, and has been struck down," answered Tom. "Get some water in a basin, and a little liquor."

When the colored man returned with the articles mentioned both boys washed the wounded man's head and bound it up with a towel. Then Tom administered a few spoonfuls of liquor. This seemed to give Peterson some strength, but he did not fully recover for some hours.

"Follow the *Peacock*," were his first rational words. "Follow the schooner *Peacock*."

"The *Peacock*?" repeated Tom. "Why should we follow her?"

"Your brother is on board." And having spoken thus, the lumberman sank again into semi-unconsciousness.

"Can he be telling the truth, or is he out of his head?" questioned Sam.

"I'm sure I don't know, Sam."

"Perhaps we had better look around for the schooner he mentioned."

"All right, I'll do so. You stay here with Aleck."

"Hadn't I better go with you?"

"No, I'll keep my eyes open," concluded Tom, and hurried away.

It was now dawn, and the early workers were just getting to their employment. Soon Tom met a couple of watchmen and hailed them.

"I am looking for the schooner *Peacock*," said he. "Do you know anything of the craft?"

"Sure, an' that's Gus Langless' boat," said one of the watchmen. "She's lying at the end of Bassoon's wharf, over yonder."

"Thank you," and Tom started away.

The wharf mentioned was a long one, and it took some time for the youth to reach the outer end. As he ran he saw a boat in the distance, moving away with all sails set. Of course he could not make out her name, but he saw that she was schooner-rigged, and felt certain she must be the craft for which he was searching.

At the end of the pier he met a dock hand, who had been resting in a nearby shed.

"Is that boat the *Peacock*?" he asked.

"Yes, sir."

"Do you know anything of the people on board?"

"I do not."

"Has she a cargo?"

"I believe not."

"You didn't see anybody going on her?"

"Hold up! Yes, I did; a young fellow and a man."

"Was the young man in a feeble state?"

Arthur M. Winfield

"He seemed to be."

"Thank you."

Tom turned away with something of a groan. "Dick must be on board of that craft, along with the Baxters. Oh, what luck we are having! Now what ought I to do next?"

His wisest move would have been to have informed the authorities, but Tom was too much upset mentally to think of that. With all speed he returned to the *Swallow*.

"The *Peacock* has sailed!" he cried. "We must follow her!"

"You are certain?" queried Sam.

"Yes, I saw her in the distance. Come, let us get after her before it is too late."

As Luke Peterson was now doing fairly well, all of the others ran on deck, and soon the *Swallow* was in pursuit of the schooner. At first but little could be seen of the *Peacock*, but when the sun came up they saw her plainly, heading toward the northwest.

"We must keep her in sight," said Tom.

"Yes, but supposing the Baxters are on board, how can we capture them?" came from Sam. "We are but three, or four at the most, counting Peterson, while that craft must carry a crew of five or six."

"We can hail some other boat to help us. The main thing is not to lose track of the rascals."

The breeze was all that could be desired, and once the shore was left behind they kept the *Peacock* in sight with ease. But, try their best, they gained but little on the larger boat.

As there was now nothing to do but to let the yacht do her best, Tom left Sam at the wheel and turned his attention to Peterson. The lumberman was now able to sit up, although very weak.

"I discovered Arnold Baxter and tracked him to the schooner's dock," he said. "His son came to the dock, and from what they said I am sure your brother is on the craft. Then they discovered me, and the father struck me down with the butt of a pistol he carried. After that all was a blank until I found myself here."

"You can be thankful you weren't killed."

"I suppose so. I shall not rest until that villain is brought to justice. But what are ye up to now, lad?"

"We are in pursuit of the *Peacock*."

"On the lake or up the river?"

"On the lake."

"Can you keep her in sight?"

"So far we seem to be holding our own."

"Good! I'd go on deck and help ye, but I feel kind o' strange-like in the legs."

"Better keep quiet for the present. We may need you later on."

"Got any firearms on board?"

"Yes, a gun and two pistols."

"Ye may want 'em afore ye git through with that crowd. They are bad ones."

"We know them thoroughly, Mr. Peterson. We have been acquainted with them for years." And then Tom told of how Dan Baxter had been the bully at Putnam Hall, and how he had run away to join his rascally father, and of how Arnold Baxter had been Mr. Rover's enemy since the days of early mining in the West.

"O' course they are carrying off your brother fer a purpose," said the lumberman. "Like as not they'll try to hit your father through him."

"I presume that is the game."

The morning wore away slowly, but as the sun mounted higher the breeze gradually died down.

The *Peacock* was the first to feel the going down of the wind, and slowly, but surely, the *Swallow* crept closer to the schooner.

But at last both vessels came to a standstill, about quarter of a mile apart.

"Now what's to do?" questioned Sam dismally.

"I reckon we can whistle for a breeze," returned his brother.

"Whistling won't do us any good. I've been wondering if we could not do some rowing in the small boat."

"Hurrah! just the thing!"

There was a small rowboat stored away on board the *Swallow*, and this was now brought forth, along with two pairs of oars.

"Gwine ter row ober, eh?" observed Aleck Pop. "Racken you dun bettah been careful wot youse do."

"We shall go armed," answered Tom.

The boys soon had the rowboat floating on the lake, and they leaped in, each with a pair of oars, and with a pistol stowed away in his pocket.

From the start those on board of the *Peacock* had been afraid that the yacht was following them, and now they were certain of it.

"Two boys putting off in a rowboat," announced Captain Langless.

"They are Tom and Sam Rover," answered Arnold Baxter, after a brief survey through a marine glass.

"How did they get to know enough to follow this craft?"

"I'm sure I don't know. But those Rover boys are slick, and always were."

"What will you do when they come up?"

"Warn them off."

"I've got an idea, dad," came from Dan.

"Well?"

"Why not get out of sight and let Captain Langless invite

Arthur M. Winfield

them on board, to look for Dick. Then we can bag them and put them with Dick."

"By Jove, that is a scheme!" exclaimed the rascally parent. "Langless, will you do it? Of course, we'll have to get out of sight until the proper moment arrives."

"But if you bag 'em, what of those left on the *Swallow*?" questioned the captain.

"There is only one man, a negro. He doesn't amount to anything."

"There may be more—one or two officers of the law."

Arnold Baxter used his glass again. "I see nobody but the darky. If there were officers at hand, I am sure they would have come along in that rowboat."

"I guess you are right about that."

"If we capture the boys the darky won't dare to follow us alone, and it may be that we can capture him, too," went on Arnold Baxter.

By this time the rowboat was drawing closer, and Arnold Baxter and Dan stepped out of sight behind the forecastle of the schooner.

A few additional words passed between Captain Langless and the Baxters, and then the owner of the *Peacock* awaited the coming of our friends, who were now almost alongside, never suspecting the trap which was set for them.

CHAPTER IX

CAUGHT IN A TRAP

"Do you see anything of the Baxters?" asked Sam, when the rowboat was within a hundred feet of the schooner.

"I thought I did before, but I don't see them now," answered Tom.

"Rowboat, ahoy!" shouted Captain Langless. "What brings you?"

"I reckon you know well enough," Tom shouted back. "We are after Dick Rover."

"Dick Rover? Who is he?"

"Your prisoner."

"Our prisoner?" The owner of the *Peacock* put on a look of surprise. "Really, you are talking in riddles."

"I don't think so. Where are Arnold Baxter and his son Dan?"

"Don't know anybody by that name."

Arthur M. Winfield

"They went on board of your boat," put in Sam.

"You must be mistaken." Captain Langless turned to his mate. "Find any stowaways on board?"

"Nary a one," was the mate's answer. "And just came up from the hold, too."

This talk perplexed Tom and Sam not a little.

Was it possible Luke Peterson had made some mistake?

"We have it on pretty good authority that the Baxters are on board of your boat, and that Dick Rover is aboard, too," said Sam.

"It's all a riddle to me," answered Captain Langless. "We are not in the business of carrying prisoners. We are bound for Sandusky for a cargo of flour."

This talk completely nonplused the boys, and they held a whispered consultation.

"I don't believe him," said Sam.

"No more do I. But what shall we do about it?"

"I'm sure I don't know."

"You can come on board and look around, if you wish," called out the owner of the schooner. "I want you to satisfy yourself that you are mistaken."

"Shall we go?" whispered Tom. "It may be a trap?"

"He seems honest enough."

"Supposing I go and you stay in the rowboat? Then, if anything happens, you can call on Aleck and Peterson for help."

So it was arranged, and in a minute more Tom was climbing up the ladder which had been thrown over the *Peacock's* side.

"Is the other young fellow coming?" asked the captain, who did not fancy this move.

"No."

The captain scowled, but said no more.

Once on deck Tom looked around him curiously, and then moved toward the companion way leading to the cabin. He felt instinctively that he was in a dangerous position. As he crossed the deck several ill-appearing sailors gazed at him curiously, but said nothing—being under strict orders from the captain to remain silent in the presence of the stranger.

The cabin of the *Peacock* was a small affair, considering the general size of the schooner, and contained but little in the shape of furniture.

Dick had been removed long before, so the apartment was empty of human occupants when Tom entered.

"Nobody here," he murmured, as he gazed around. "What foolishness to come, anyway! The Baxters could easily hide on me, if they wanted to."

He was about to leave the cabin when a form darkened the companion way, and Arnold Baxter appeared.

"Silence!" commanded the man, and pointed a pistol at

Tom's head.

The sight of the rascal startled the youth and the look on Baxter's face caused him to shiver.

"So you are here, after all," he managed to say.

"Silence!" repeated Arnold Baxter, "unless you want to be shot."

"Where is my brother Dick?"

Before Arnold Baxter could reply Dan put in an appearance, carrying a pair of handcuffs.

"Now, we'll get square with you, Tom Rover," said the bully harshly.

"What do you intend to do?"

"Make you a prisoner. Hold out your hands."

"And if I refuse?"

"You won't refuse," put in Arnold Baxter, and, lowering his pistol, he leaped behind Tom and caught him by the arms. At the same time Dan attacked the lad in front and poor Tom was soon handcuffed. Then he was led out of the cabin by a rear way, a door was opened, and he was thrust into the blackness of the hold. But ere this was accomplished he let out one long, loud cry for help which reached Sam's ears quite plainly.

"Hi! what are you doing to my brother?" ejaculated the younger Rover. He had brought the rowboat close up alongside the schooner.

"I don't know what's up," answered the mate of the *Peacock*. "Better come aboard and see."

"He has fallen down the hatchway!" cried Captain Langless. "Poor chap! he's hurt himself quite badly." And he disappeared, as if going to Tom's assistance.

If Sam had been in a quandary before, he was doubly so now. Had Tom really fallen, or had he been attacked?

"I can't leave him alone," he thought, and without further hesitation leaped up the side of the schooner with the agility of a cat.

It was a fatal movement, for scarcely had he reached the deck when he was pounced upon by Captain Langless and held fast until Arnold Baxter appeared.

"Let me go!" cried Sam, but his protest proved of no avail. A lively scuffle followed, but the lad was no match for the men, and in the end he found himself handcuffed and thrown into the hold beside Tom.

"Tie the rowboat fast to the stern," ordered Arnold Baxter, and this was done.

The going down of the wind was only temporary, and now a slight breeze sprang up.

"We are in luck!" said the captain of the schooner.

"We must keep away from the yacht," returned Arnold Baxter.

Soon the schooner's sails were filling and she continued on her course, dragging the small boat behind her. Aleck Pop saw the movement and grew much perplexed.

Arthur M. Winfield

"Dat don't look right to me, nohow!" he muttered. "'Pears lak da was bein' tuk along sumway!"

Aleck was not much of a sailor, but he had been out enough to know how to handle the yacht under ordinary circumstances, and now he did his best to follow the *Peacock*.

With the glass he watched eagerly for the reappearance of Sam and Tom, and his face became a study when fully half an hour passed and they failed to show themselves.

"Da is in trouble, suah!" he told himself. "Now wot's dis yeah niggah to do?"

He lashed the wheel fast and sought advice from Luke Peterson, who was feeling stronger every minute. The burly lumberman shook his head dubiously.

"In trouble for certain," was his comment. "Didn't hear any pistol shots, did ye?"

"Didn't heah nuffin, sah."

"They wouldn't remain on board of that craft of their own free will."

"Don't specs da would, sah. De question is, sah: wot's to do?" And Aleck scratched his woolly head thoughtfully.

"I don't know, excepting to keep the schooner in sight, if possible, and see if something doesn't turn up. If you sight a steamer or a steam tug let me know, and I'll try to get help."

So it was arranged, and Aleck returned to the wheel. The *Swallow* was going along smoothly, and he did what he could to make the sails draw as much as possible. Peterson now discovered the medicine chest of the yacht, and from this got another dose of liquor, which afforded him the temporary strength of which he was in so much need.

The coming of night found the two vessels far out upon the waters of Lake Erie and nearly half a mile apart. Peterson now came on deck, to keep an eye on things while Aleck prepared supper. It promised to remain clear, but, as there would be no moon, Peterson was afraid that they would lose sight of the *Peacock* in the gathering darkness.

Supper was soon served, the lumberman eating first, and then Aleck cleared away the few dishes and tidied up generally. The colored man was much downcast.

"Fust it was Dick, an' now it am de whole t'ree of 'em," he remarked. "I'se afraid dar is gwine ter be a bad endin' to dis yeah trip."

"We will have to take what comes," answered Peterson. "But I have taken a fancy to those boys, and I'll stick by you to the end."

Slowly the darkness of night settled over the waters of the lake, and with the going down of the sun the stars came forth, one after another. During the last few hours several sail had been seen at a distance, but none had come close enough to be hailed.

"We are going to lose her in the darkness, after all," announced the lumberman, at about eight o'clock. "It's hard for me to see her, even now."

Half an hour later the *Peacock* disappeared in the gloom, and the chase, for the time being, came to an end.

CHAPTER X

THE ESCAPE FROM THE HOLD

"Sam, is that you?"

"Yes."

"We are trapped!"

"It looks like it—or rather feels like it. I can't see a thing."

"Nor I. Did you find out anything about Dick?"

"No."

A groan came from the opposite end of the hold.

"Here I am. How in the world did you get here?"

"Dick, after all!" ejaculated Tom, and there was a slight trace of joy in his tone. "Are you O. K., old man?"

"Hardly. They dosed me with drugs until my mind is topsy-turvy."

"I'm glad you are alive," came from Sam. "Where are you?"

"Here, lying on a couple of boxes. Look out how you move about, or you may hurt yourselves."

Handcuffed as they were, Tom and Sam felt their way along through the dark hold until they reached their elder brother's side. They grasped his hands warmly.

"I'm glad we are together again, even if we are prisoners," remarked Tom, and this was his younger brother's sentiment, too.

"How did you get here?" asked Dick, and each told his story from beginning to end, and then the elder Rover had to relate his own adventures.

"I knew that old doctor wasn't telling the truth," burst out Tom. "Oh, but won't we have an account to settle with all of those chaps, if ever we get out of this scrape."

"Don't let us hurrah until we are out of the woods," added Dick soberly. "We are in the hands of a desperate gang, to my way of reasoning."

"The Baxters are certainly bad enough."

"And any boat captain who would go into this game with them is probably just as bad. Whom did you leave on the yacht?"

"Aleck, and the lumberman who was on the raft with you."

"I wonder if they will follow this schooner?"

No one could answer this question, and for several minutes there was a silence. During that time they heard heavy footsteps cross and recross the deck, but that was all. Presently the schooner began to rock slightly.

"The wind is coming up," said Tom. "We are moving ahead again."

"That's bad for us—if the schooner manages to run away from the yacht," rejoined Dick.

Soon the motion of the *Peacock* showed that the schooner was bowling along rapidly. They heard the creaking of tackle as additional sails were hoisted, and felt certain that the craft was making the best run at her command.

The hold had not been opened up for a long time, consequently the air was foul as well as stifling from the heat.

"I'd give something for some fresh air," said Sam. "How is it with you, Dick?"

"I want fresh air and a drink of water. I am as dry as a bale of cotton."

"Haven't they given you anything since you came on board?" asked Tom.

"Not a thing."

"The inhuman wretches! Oh, I wish I had Dan Baxter here —I'd punch his head good for him."

"Ditto the head of his rascally father," returned Dick. "I would like to know just where they intend to take me—or rather all of us, now. They certainly can't expect to keep us on board this craft."

"Perhaps they'll ship us to Canada."

"Hardly, since they couldn't land on the Canadian shore without an inspection of the vessel."

"They have some plan up their sleeve, that's certain."

Slowly the hours wore away, until all sounds on deck ceased, and they knew it must be well along in the night. Still the schooner kept on her course.

All of the boys had been working at their bonds, but without success. They wished they had a light, but neither Sam nor Tom had a match, and Dick's pockets were entirely bare. Tom and Sam were likewise minus their pistols, Arnold Baxter having taken the weapons away before placing them in the hold.

The night proved to be a truly horrible one for the boys, for the hold was overrun with rats, who became altogether too familiar. At first one of the pests ran over Tom's legs.

"A rat!" he cried. "Hi, scat!" And the frisky rodent scampered off, but speedily returned, followed by several others. After that they had a lively time of it for half an hour, when the rats left them as suddenly as they had appeared.

The storm, and their various adventures, had tired the boys out, and soon, in spite of the surroundings, one after another fell into a light doze. The sleep did all of them good, especially Dick, who declared on awakening that he felt almost as well as ever.

"Only I'm as hungry as a bear," he added.

"Ditto myself," came from Tom. "I move we try to break out of this dingy hole."

"All right; but where shall we break to?" put in Sam. "I can't see much more than I could last night."

The matter was talked over, and presently they scattered, to feel along the ribbed walls of the hold.

For a long time nobody felt anything of importance, but at last Sam let out a soft cry:

"I've found something of a door!"

"Good for you," answered Tom. "Can you open it?"

"No, there seems to be a bar or something on the other side."

The others rejoined the youngest Rover, and made out the door quite plainly, for there was a broad crack at the top and at the side opposite the hinges. There was a bar, true enough.

"If we had something that we could slip into that crack, we might move the bar," observed Dick.

"I slipped on a sheet of tin a while ago," said Tom. "Perhaps I can find that."

His hunt was successful, and soon they had the tin in the crack under the bar. The latter gave way with ease, and then they pulled the door open. Beyond was the passageway leading to the cabin.

"Now what's the next movement?" whispered Sam.

"Let us try to arm ourselves first of all," answered Dick. "Then, if we are cornered again, we may be able to make some kind of favorable terms."

He tiptoed his way into the cabin and found it deserted. On the table rested the remains of a breakfast served to several people, and he picked up half a loaf of bread and put it in the pocket of his jacket. Several boiled eggs followed.

On one of the walls of the cabin hung two old-fashioned swords and a brace of pistols. Without hesitation he took all of the weapons and returned with them to his brothers.

"Here are pistols and swords, and something to eat," he said. "There seems to be nobody around, so you can come into the cabin, if you wish."

All entered the compartment. Both water and a little coffee were handy, and they made a hasty repast. While eating, Tom hunted around the room and also looked into an adjoining stateroom. In the latter place he found a bunch of keys on a nail.

"If only one of 'em fits these handcuffs," he murmured, and they tried the keys without delay. One did fit, and in a few seconds they were free of their fetters.

"Now 'lay on, MacDuff!'" quoted Tom, as he swung aloft one of the swords. "We'll give them a warm reception, eh?"

"We'll do nothing of the kind," replied Dick hastily. "In this case silence is the better part of valor. We'll lay low until the time comes to make a move."

"What, do you mean to go back to the hold?" asked Sam.

"We may as well, for the present. It is broad daylight now. Perhaps we can escape at night."

"Do you suppose they took our rowboat along?" came from Tom.

"I shouldn't wonder. We can—Hist! somebody is coming!" Dick was right; Captain Langless was descending the companion way. On tiptoes the three boys hurried to the door leading to the hold. As they flung it back they found themselves confronted by Arnold Baxter and Dan.

CHAPTER XI

GAINING A POINT

The sudden turn of affairs chagrined the Rover boys greatly, and for the moment none of them knew what to say.

Arnold Baxter and Dan grinned at the trio sarcastically, and the bully was the first to break the silence.

"Didn't get away that time, did you?" he sneered.

"Ha! so they are here!" came from Captain Langless, who had just stepped into the cabin. "And without the handcuffs, too."

"Let us alone," cried Tom hotly. "If you touch me again, I'll shoot somebody." And so speaking, he raised one of the pistols taken from the cabin wall.

His aim was at Dan, and the bully fell back with a cry of terror, for, as old readers know, Dan was a coward at heart.

"Don't—don't shoot!" he faltered. "Don't!"

"My pistols!" burst out the captain of the *Peacock*, in a rage. "Hand those weapons over to me, do you hear?"

He took several steps forward, when Dick brought him to a halt by raising one of the swords.

It was a dramatic scene, of intense interest to all concerned. Arnold Baxter gazed at the armed youths in alarm, and Captain Langless grated his teeth.

"This is foolishness," said the owner of the schooner, after a painful pause. "If you try to fight you'll only get into worse trouble. We are, all told, ten to three, and the best thing you can do is to throw down those arms and submit."

"We won't submit," came from Sam, with a boldness which was astonishing in one of his years. His stirring adventures in Africa and in the West accounted for much of this valor.

"We are not going to remain on this vessel," said Dick. "And if you try to detain us further somebody will get hurt."

"You scamp!" fumed Arnold Baxter, and looked at the elder Rover as if to annihilate him with a glance. But Dick remained undaunted, and gradually Arnold Baxter fell back a few steps.

It must be confessed that the Rover boys felt far from comfortable. Here were two of the enemy on one side and one on the other, cutting off their escape in both directions. More than this, Captain Langless now raised his voice, and presently several rough-looking sailors came rushing into the cabin.

"Leave the hold," cried the owner of the schooner to the Baxters. "I reckon I know how to manage 'em."

Arnold Baxter understood, and at once took his son by the arm. The pair had come down into the hold by means of a ladder lowered through the forward hatchway. Now they ran for the ladder, mounted, and drew it up after them. Then the hatch was closed down as before.

In the meantime Captain Langless whispered to one of his sailors, and the tar ran to one of the staterooms and returned with an old-fashioned seven-shooter, fully a foot and a half long.

"Now get back there," ordered the owner of the schooner. "I won't have any more fooling."

"If you shoot, so will I," said Tom quickly.

"And so will I," added Sam.

"We had better have no bloodshed," continued the captain, trying to control himself. "Behave yourselves, and you'll be treated all right. Kick up a muss, and it will go hard with you."

"What do you intend to do with us?" questioned Dick curiously.

"You'll have to ask your friend Arnold Baxter about that."

"He is no friend of ours!" cried Tom. "He is our worst enemy—and you know it."

"If you behave yourself I'll see to it that no harm befalls you," continued Captain Langless. "I'm sorry I mixed up in this affair, but now I am in it I'm going to see it through."

"You are carrying us off against our will."

The owner of the *Peacock* shrugged his shoulders.

"You'll have to talk that over with Baxter and his son."

"You've been starving us."

"We were just going to furnish you with breakfast and a small keg of water."

"We don't want to stay in that foul-smelling hold," put in Sam. "It is enough to make a fellow sick."

"If you'll promise to behave yourselves, we may let you on deck part of the time."

"You'd better," grumbled Tom. He hardly knew what to say, and his brothers were in an equal quandary.

"Come, throw down your arms and we'll give you breakfast here in the cabin," continued Captain Langless. "You won't find me such a bad chap to deal with, when once you know me. You look like decent sort of fellows, and if you do the right thing I'll promise to see to it that the Baxters do the square thing, too. We'll be better off on a friendly footing than otherwise."

The owner of the *Peacock* spoke earnestly, and it must be admitted that he meant a large part of what he said. The manliness of the Rover boys pleased him, and he could not help but contrast it with the cowardice of the bully, Dan. Perhaps, too, behind it all, he was a bit sick of the job he had undertaken. He knew that he had virtually helped to kidnap the boys, and, if caught, this would mean a long term of imprisonment.

Dick looked at his two brothers, wondering what they would have to say. He realized that, after all, they were in a hopeless minority and were bound to lose in a hand-to-hand struggle.

"We may as well try them," he whispered. "If we fight, one

of us may get killed."

They talked among themselves for several minutes, and then Dick turned to the captain.

"We'll submit for the present," he said. "But, mind you, we expect to be treated like gentlemen."

"And you will be treated as such," answered Captain Langless, glad that there would be no struggle. "Come into the cabin and stack those weapons in the corner. They were never meant for anything but wall decorations," and he laughed somewhat nervously.

The three lads entered the cabin and put down the weapons. They kept their eyes on the captain and his men, but there was no move to molest them.

"You can go," said Captain Langless to the sailors. "And, Wilson, send the cook here for orders."

The sailors departed, and with something of a grim smile on his furrowed face the owner of the *Peacock* dropped into a seat near the companionway door. He had just started to speak again when there was a noise outside and Arnold Baxter appeared.

"Have you subdued the rascals?" he questioned hastily.

"Reckon I have," was the slow answer, "Leas'wise, they have thrown down their weapons."

"Then why don't you handcuff them again, the rats!"

"We are no rats, and I'll trouble you to be civil," returned Dick firmly.

Arthur M. Winfield

"Ha! I'll show you!" howled Arnold Baxter, and would have rushed at Dick had not the captain interposed.

"Hold on, sir," were the words of the ship's owner. "We have called a truce. They have promised to behave themselves if we treat them squarely, and so there are to be no more back-bitings."

"But—er—" Arnold Baxter was so astonished he could scarcely speak. "You are not going to put them in the hold?"

"Not for the present."

"They will run away."

"How can they, when we are out of sight of land?"

"They ought to be chained down."

"Supposing you let me be the judge of that, Mr. Baxter. I promised to do certain things for you. If I do them, you'll have no cause to complain."

"Have you decided to take these boys' part?" ejaculated Arnold Baxter, turning pale.

"I have made up my mind that treating them like beasts won't do any good."

"They don't deserve it."

"Don't deserve what?"

"To be well treated. They are—are—"

"Young gentlemen," finished Tom. "The captain knows gentlemen when he sees them, even if you don't."

"Don't talk to me, Tom Rover."

"I will talk whenever I please. I am not your slave."

"But you are in my power, don't forget that."

At this moment the cook of the schooner appeared.

"What's wanted?" he asked of the captain.

"Bring some breakfast for these three young gentlemen," said Captain Langless. "Some fresh coffee and bread and some fried eggs and potatoes."

At this order Arnold Baxter stood fairly aghast. "You are going to let them dine here?" he gasped.

"I am."

"But—but you must be crazy. They will—er—think they are running the ship!"

"No, they won't. Leave them to me, and I'm sure we will get along all right. Come, let us go on deck."

"What! and leave them alone?"

"I will send a man down to see that they don't get into mischief."

"But I don't like this turn of affairs," stammered Arnold Baxter. He was half afraid the captain was going back on him.

"It's all right; come," answered the owner of the *Peacock*; and a moment later both men quitted the cabin.

CHAPTER XII

A DINNER OF IMPORTANCE

"The captain isn't such a bad fellow, after all," observed Sam, when the three Rovers were left to themselves.

"He certainly isn't a brute," answered Dick. "But about being bad, that's another story."

"He's got an awfully shrewd face," put in Tom. "But I'm mighty glad he turned old Baxter down. That villain would ride over us roughshod."

"I think, all told, we have gained a point," continued Dick. "It's something to be treated decently, even if you are a prisoner. The question is, how long will we be caged up on board of the schooner?"

"I would like to know if the *Swallow* is in sight," said Tom. "Wonder if I can't slip up the companion way and find out?"

He arose from the seat into which he had dropped, but before he could gain the doorway a sailor appeared and waved him back. Then the sailor took the seat the captain had occupied by the door.

"Are you sent to spy on us?" demanded Tom,

"I was sent to see that you didn't cut up any tricks," answered the tar. He was terribly crosseyed, but appeared to be rather good-natured. "You mustn't go on deck without the captain's permission."

"Can't we have any fresh air?"

"You'll have to ask the captain about that He said I was to watch you while you had breakfast, and keep you and those other folks from quarreling."

"What other folks, the Baxters?"

"Yes."

No more was said, and soon the cook appeared with a pot full of newly made coffee and a trayful of other things. The hasty lunch had been a scanty one, and it did not interfere with the boys' appetites for what was now set before them.

"This is all right," observed Sam, when he had almost finished eating. "We couldn't have a better meal on the *Swallow*." He turned to the sailor. "Is the yacht still in sight?"

He spoke carelessly, but the tar knew how much he was interested and smiled suggestively.

"No sail of any kind in sight."

"Where are we bound?"

"You'll have to ask the captain about that"

"Do you mean to say you don't know?"

The sailor nodded. "We follow orders, we do, and that's all," he observed, and then they could get nothing more out of him.

The boys took their time, yet the meal was finished inside of half an hour. They were just getting up from the table when Captain Langless reappeared.

"Well, how did the breakfast suit?" he asked.

"First-rate," returned Dick. "Now, if you don't mind, we would like to go on deck."

"You may do so under one condition."

"And that is—?"

"That you will go below again when ordered by me."

At this both Tom and Sam cut wry faces.

"You are rather hard on us," said Dick slowly.

"On the contrary, I think I am treating you generously. The Baxters wish to handcuff you and put you back into the hold."

There was a pause, and then the boys agreed, if allowed to go on deck, to go below again whenever the captain wished.

"But, remember, we are going to get away if we can," added Dick.

"All right, get away—if you can," rejoined Captain Langless. "If you go overboard you'll be in for a long swim, I can tell you that."

It felt good to get into the bright sunshine once more, and the boys tumbled up to the deck without ceremony. As soon as they had quitted the cabin the captain put away the weapons at hand, locking them in a closet.

As the sailor had said, no other craft was in sight, and on every hand stretched the calm waters of Lake Erie as far as eye could reach. The course was northwest, and Dick rightfully guessed that they were heading for the Detroit River. There was a stiff breeze blowing and, with every sail set, the *Peacock* was making rapid headway.

It was not long before Dan Baxter came up to them. The bully's face was dark and threatening, yet he did not dare say much, for Captain Langless had given him warning that the prisoners must not be molested.

"I suppose you think it a fine thing to be up here," he began.

"It will be if we don't get too much of you." replied Tom bluntly. "I suppose you would give a good deal to be on land."

"Not particularly. We enjoy sailing. If not, we wouldn't have been out in our yacht/'

"Where were you bound?"

"That was our business, Baxter."

"Oh, if you don't want to tell me, you needn't," growled the bully, and walked away.

"I'll wager he and his father have had a row with Captain Langless," observed Dick. "Otherwise he wouldn't be half so meek."

"I wish we could win Captain Langless over to our side," put in Sam suddenly, struck by the idea. "Do you suppose it could be done if we paid him well?"

"I'd hate to buy him off," said Tom.

"But it might be best," said Dick slowly. "We don't know what the Baxters may have in store for us."

"It's pretty plain to me what they want to do. They are going to hold us prisoners until father signs off his rights to that mining claim."

"And if father won't sign off?"

"Then they'll treat us pretty badly."

"Perhaps they'll kill us."

"We can sound Captain Langless—it won't do any harm."

"But you mustn't let the Baxters get an inkling of what is up."

For the present the captain was not in sight, having retired to the stern to consult Arnold Baxter upon several points. They remained on deck until noon, when the cook called them to dinner in the cabin. They found they were to dine with Captain Langless.

"I asked the Baxters to join us, but they declined," he observed, as they sat down. "Now I am not so high-toned."

"You mean you are not such a fool," returned Dick. "For myself, I am glad they are staying away. My meal would be spoiled if I had to eat with them."

"They are very bitter against you, that's certain," went on the owner of the schooner smoothly. "They want me to do all sorts of mean things. But I have declined. I am playing a game with them, but I want to do it as be comes a man."

Dick looked around, to see that no outsider was within earshot. "Why do you play the game with them, Captain Langless?" he whispered.

The owner of the schooner frowned.

"Well, one must make a living, if you want an answer," he returned shortly.

"True, but you might make a living more honestly."

"By helping us, for instance," added Tom.

"By helping you?"

"Yes, by helping us," resumed Dick.

"I must say, lads, I don't quite understand you." The captain looked at them sharply, as if anxious for either to proceed.

"Let us review the situation," continued the eldest of the Rovers. "In the first place, we take it that you have been hired by the Baxters to do a certain thing."

"Granted."

"The Baxters have promised to pay you for your work and for the use of your vessel."

"Granted again."

Arthur M. Winfield

"You are running on dangerous ground, and if you get tripped up it means a long term of imprisonment."

"You are a clever fellow, Rover, and your school training does you credit. However, I don't know as any of us expect to get tripped up."

"No criminal does until he is caught."

"There may be something in that. But I am willing to take my chances. As the old saying goes: 'Nothing ventured, nothing gained.'"

"But wouldn't you rather venture on the right side?"

"You want me to come to terms; is that it?"

"We do. We can make it worth your while, if you will help us and help bring the Baxters to justice. Do you know that Arnold Baxter is an escaped convict, who got out of a New York prison on a forged pardon?"

"No, I know very little of the man."

"He is a bad one, and his son is little better. Standing in with them is a serious business. I don't know much about you, but you don't look like a man who is bad by choice."

At this the captain of the *Peacock* let out a light laugh. "You talk as if you were a man of deep experience instead of a mere boy."

"I have had some experience, especially with bad folks—not only in this country, but in Africa, so that gives me an age not counted by years. To my mind it seems that a man ought to be more willing to make money honestly than dishonestly."

A long silence followed this speech.

"Tell me what you have to offer," said the captain, and leaned back in his chair to listen.

Arthur M. Winfield

CHAPTER XIII

PRISONERS THREE

It was easy to see that Captain Langless was "feeling his way," as the saying is, and Dick felt that he must go slow or he might spoil everything. Criminals are of all shades and degrees, and look at affairs in a different light from honest men. It is said that some would rather be dishonest than honest, and Dick did not yet know how the owner of the *Peacock* stood on that point.

"Perhaps you had better tell us first what Arnold Baxter has offered you," said the elder Rover, as he looked the owner of the schooner squarely in the eyes.

"Well, he has offered considerable, if his schemes go through."

"And if they fail you get nothing."

"I am a good loser—so I shan't complain."

"Supposing I was to offer you several hundred dollars if you saw us safe on shore."

"How can you offer any money? You haven't got it with you, have you?"

"No. But I could get the money, and what I promised to pay I would pay."

"But several hundred dollars wouldn't be enough."

"If you helped to bring the Baxters to justice we might make it a thousand dollars," put in Tom, who was now as anxious as Dick to bring the captain to terms.

At the mention of a thousand dollars the eyes of Captain Langless glistened. The sum was not large, but it was sufficient to interest him. He had already received three hundred dollars from Arnold Baxter, as a guarantee of good faith, so to speak, but there was no telling how much more he could expect from that individual. If he could obtain thirteen hundred dollars all told, and get out of the affair on the safe side, he might be doing well.

"How would you pay this thousand dollars?" he asked.

"Our father would pay it. He is a fairly rich man, and anxious to see Arnold Baxter returned to prison."

"To get the man out of his path?"

"Partly that, and partly to see justice done. Come, what do you say?"

Before the captain could answer there came a call down the companion way.

"Two vessels in sight—a schooner and a steam tug," announced a sailor.

"Coming this way?" asked the master of the schooner.

"Aye, sir."

Arthur M. Winfield

Captain Langless arose at once.

"I will have to ask you to step into the hold again," he said politely, but firmly. "I will talk over what you have offered later."

He motioned to the passageway leading to the hold. Sam was on the point of objecting, but Dick silenced him with a look.

"All right, we'll go," grumbled Tom. "But I'm going to take the dessert with me," and he took up a bowl of rice pudding and a spoon. Dick followed with a pitcher of water and a glass, at which the captain had to grin. As soon as they were in the hold the owner of the schooner bolted the door and fixed it so that it might not again be opened from the inside.

"Two ships in sight!" cried Sam, when they were alone. "We ought to have made a dash for liberty."

"It wouldn't have helped us," answered his oldest brother. "Those vessels must be some distance away, and before they came up we would be down here, handcuffed, and in disgrace with the captain. If we treat him right, we may win him over and finish the Baxters' game."

Sitting in the darkness they took their time about eating the rice pudding, and Dick placed the water where it could be found when wanted. Then they listened for the approach of the two vessels which the lookout had sighted.

Yet hour after hour went by and nothing of importance reached their ears. The vessels came up and passed them, and then the *Peacock* turned in for the mouth of the Detroit River. Soon the boys knew, by the steam whistles and other sounds, that the schooner was approaching some sort of harbor.

A dreary evening and night followed. The *Peacock* came to a standstill, and they heard the sails come down and the anchors dropped. But nobody came to them, and they had to sink to rest supperless. They remained awake until after midnight, then dozed off one after another.

When they awoke a surprise awaited them. The hold was lit up by the rays of a bright lantern hung on a hook near the door leading to the cabin passageway. Below the lantern stood a tray filled with eatables, and near at hand was a bucket of fresh water and half a dozen newspapers and magazines.

"By Jinks, this is not so bad!" observed Tom. "We are to have breakfast, that's certain."

"And reading to occupy our spare time," added Sam.

Dick, however, looked at the layout with a fallen face. "I don't like it," he said. "This looks too much as if the captain and the others meant to keep us here for some time."

"I suppose that's so," came from Tom, and then he, too, looked crestfallen.

"Well, let us make the best of it," said Sam, and began to eat, and the others did the same. Since time seemed no object they ate slowly, in the meantime reviewing the situation from every possible standpoint, but without arriving at any satisfactory conclusion.

They had allowed their watches to run down, so there was no telling what time it was. But at last a faint streak of sunshine, coming through a seam in the deck, told that it must be near noon. Yet no one came near them, and all was as silent, close at hand, as a tomb, although in the distance they heard an occasional steam whistle or other sound common to a great city.

There was nothing in the hold by which to reach the hatchway, but, growing weary of waiting, Tom dragged a box hither and asked Dick and Sam to stand upon it. Then he climbed on their shoulders, to find his head directly against the beams of the deck. He pushed with all of his strength on the hatch, to find it battened down on the outside.

"Stumped!" he cried laconically, and leaped to the floor of the hold. "We are prisoners and no mistake."

After this they went back to the door leading to the cabin. But this likewise could not be moved, and in the end they sat down a good deal discouraged.

It was well toward night when they heard a noise at the door. As they leaped up, expecting to see the Baxters or Captain Langless, the barrier opened and the cook of the schooner appeared, backed up by two of the sailors. The cook had another trayful of food, which he passed to Dick in silence, taking the other tray in exchange.

"Where is Captain Langless?" asked Tom.

"Can't come now," answered the cook.

"Then send the Baxters here."

"They can't come either."

"Have they gone ashore?" questioned Dick.

"I can't answer any questions," and the cook started to back out.

"Who is in charge? We must see somebody."

"I am in charge," said a rough voice, and now the mate of the schooner thrust himself forward. "You had better be quiet until the cap'n gits back."

"Then he has gone ashore?"

"Yes, if you must know."

"And the Baxters with him."

"Yes, but all hands will be back soon."

"Are we in Detroit harbor?"

"Yes."

"Then I'm for escaping!" shouted Tom, and taking up the water pitcher he aimed it at the mate's head. The blow struck fairly, and the sailor went down, partly stunned. Seeing the success of his move Tom leaped for the passageway, and Dick and Sam followed their brother.

CHAPTER XIV

DICK MAKES HIS ESCAPE

There are times when a movement made on the spur of the moment is more successful than one which is premeditated. The enemy is taken completely off guard and does not realize what is happening until it is over.

It was so in the present instance. The mate of the *Peacock* was a tough customer and a heavy-built man, and the men behind him were also large, and none of the three had imagined that the boys would really undertake to combat them.

As the mate went down Tom leaped directly on top of him, thus holding him to the floor for the moment, and then struck out for the nearest man, hitting him in the chin. Then Dick came to his brother's aid with a blow that reached the sailor's ear, and he too fell back.

But the third man had a second to think, and he retaliated by a blow which nearly lifted poor Tom off his feet. But before he could strike out a second time, Sam, with the nimbleness of a monkey, darted in and caught him by one leg. Dick saw the movement, gave the sailor a shove, and the tar pitched headlong in the passageway.

The opening was now tolerably clear, and away went the three boys for the cabin, gaining the compartment before any of the men could follow. The door to the companion way was open, and up the steps they flew with all the speed at their command. They heard the sailors yell at them and use language unfit to print, but paid no heed. Their one thought was to put distance between themselves and those who wished to keep them prisoners.

"Stop! stop!" roared the mate. "Stop, or it will be the worse for you!"

"I guess we know what we are doing!" panted Tom. "Come on!" And he caught Sam by the arm.

The deck gained, they gave a hasty look around. The schooner was lying at anchor about a hundred yards from shore, at a short distance above the busy portion of the city.

"There ought to be a small boat handy," said Dick, leading the way to the stern.

"We can't wait for a boat," answered Sam. "Let us swim for it. Perhaps somebody will come and pick us up." And without further ado he leaped overboard. Seeing this, his brothers did likewise, and all three struck out boldly for the nearest dock.

It was a risky thing to do, with all their clothing on, but each was a good swimmer and the weather had made the water very warm. On they went, keeping as closely together as possible.

"Are you coming back?" furiously yelled the mate, as he reached the rail and shook his fist at them.

To this none of the boys made reply.

Arthur M. Winfield

"If you don't come back I'll shoot at you," went on the man.

"Do you think he will shoot?" asked Sam, in alarm.

"No," answered Dick. "We are too close to the city, and there are too many people who would hear the shot."

"A boat is putting off from the shore," said Tom, a second later. "It contains three persons."

"Captain Langless and the Baxters!" burst out Dick. "Dive, and swim as hard as you can down the stream."

All promptly dove, and the weight of their clothing kept them under as long as they pleased to remain. When they came up they heard the mate yelling frantically to those in the boat, who did not at once comprehend the turn affairs had taken.

But when they saw the boys they began to row toward them with all swiftness.

"We must recapture them," cried Arnold Baxter. "If they get away, our cake will be dough."

"Then row as hard as you can," replied Captain Langless. He was at one pair of oars while Arnold Baxter was at another. Dan sat in the bow.

Slowly, but surely, the craft drew closer to the Rover boys, until it was less than a hundred feet off. Then it was seen that the lads had separated and were moving in three directions. Dick had ordered this.

"If we separate, they won't catch all of us," were his words. "And whoever escapes can inform the authorities."

On pushed the boys, striving as never before to gain the shore before the rowboat should come up to them.

The small craft headed first for Tom, and presently it glided close to him. He promptly dove, but when he came up Captain Langless caught him by the hair.

"It's no use, lad," said the captain firmly, and despite his struggles hauled him on board.

"Let me go!" roared Tom and kicked out lively. But the captain continued to hold him down, while Arnold Baxter now headed the boat toward Sam.

Sam was almost exhausted, for the weight of his wet garments was beginning to tell upon him. As the rowboat came closer he also thought to dive, but the effort almost cost him his life. He came up half unconscious, and only realized in a dim, uncertain way what was happening.

But the capture of Tom and his younger brother had taken time, and now those in the rowboat saw that Dick was almost to shore. To take him, therefore, was out of the question.

"We'll have to let him go," said Captain Langless. "The quicker the *Peacock* gets out of this the better."

"Yes, but if he gets away he'll make the ship no end of trouble," returned Arnold Baxter. "I've half a mind to fire at him," and he drew a pistol.

"No! no! I won't have it," cried the captain sternly. "To the schooner, and the quicker the better."

Holding Tom, he made the Baxters turn the boat about and row to the *Peacock*. The mate was waiting for him, and it did not take long to get on board. The mate wished to explain matters, but Captain Lawless would not listen.

"Another time, Cadmus," he said sharply. "Into the hold with them, and see they don't get away again. We must up sail and anchor without the loss of a minute. That boy who got away is going to make trouble for us."

"Aye, aye, sir!" said Cadmus, and dragged the unfortunates away to the hatch. He dropped both down without ceremony, and then saw to it that hatch and door were tightly closed and made fast.

In a few minutes the anchors were up and the sails hoisted, and the *Peacock* was steering straight up Lake St. Clair toward the St. Clair River. To reach Lake Huron the schooner would have to cover a distance of seventy-five to eighty miles, and the captain wondered if this could be done ere the authorities got on their track.

"Once on Lake Huron we will be safe enough," he observed to Arnold Baxter. "I know the lake well, and know of half a dozen islands near the Canadian shore where we will be safe in hiding."

"But that boy may telegraph to St. Clair or Port Huron, or some other point, and have the *Peacock* held up," answered Arnold Baxter.

"We've got to run that risk," was the grim reply. "If we get caught, I'll have an account to settle with Cadmus."

A while later the mate and the sailors who had been with him were called into the cabin, so that Captain Langless might hear what they had to say. The mate told a long story of how the boys had broken open the door leading to the cabin, with a crowbar, obtained from he knew not where, and had fought them with the bar and with a club and a pistol. There had been a fierce struggle, but the lads had slipped away like eels. The sailors corroborated the mate's tale, and added that the boys had fought like demons.

"I'll fix them for that," said Arnold Baxter, when he heard the account. "They'll find out who is master before I get through with them."

But this did not suit Captain Langless, who had not forgotten his talk with the Rovers at the dinner table. If it looked as if he was going to be cornered, he thought that a compromise with Tom and Sam would come in very handy.

"You mustn't mistreat the boys," he said, when Cadmus and the other sailors were gone. "It won't help your plot any, and it will only cause more trouble."

"You seem to be taking the affair out of my hands," growled Arnold Baxter.

"I know I am running a larger risk than you," answered the captain. "I own this craft, and if she is confiscated I'll be the loser."

"But see what I have offered you."

"Yes, if we win out, as the saying goes. But things won't be so nice if we lose, will they?"

"I don't intend to lose. I have a scheme on hand for getting to Lake Huron before to-morrow morning."

"By what means?"

"Hire a large and swift tug to haul the *Peacock*. We can make splendid time, considering that the schooner is without a cargo."

"Who is going to pay the towing bill?"

"How much will it be?"

"The kind of tug you want will cost about fifty dollars."

"All right then, I'll pay the bill."

The idea pleased the captain, and the bargain was struck then and there.

Half an hour later a tug was sighted and hailed, and the captain told a story of a "rush job" waiting for him at Port Huron. A bargain was struck for the towing, and soon a hawser was cast over to the schooner and the race for Lake Huron began.

CHAPTER XV

WHAT THE LAME MAN KNEW

Dick was not aware that his brothers had been captured until some hours after the sailing of the schooner. He headed for a part of the river where several small craft were moving about, and was just about to climb up the spiling of one of the docks when a lighter hit him and knocked him senseless.

"We've struck a boy!" shouted a man on the lighter, and then rushed forward with a boathook. As soon as he caught sight of Dick he fished the youth from the water and hurried ashore with him.

The shock had not been a heavy one, but the lad was weak from swimming with his clothes on, and he lay like a log on the flooring of the dock. This alarmed the men from the lighter, and they hastily carried him to a nearby drug store and summoned a doctor. From the drug store he was removed to the hospital.

When he was strong enough to go about his business he found it was night Yet he lost no time in making his way to the docks, on a search for his brothers.

The search was, of course, useless, and much depressed in

Arthur M. Winfield

spirits he found himself, at sunrise, on the waterfront, seated on the stringpiece of one of the long piers.

"They must have either been captured or drowned," he mused dismally. "And the *Peacock* is gone, too. What shall I do next?"

It was far from an easy question to answer, and he sat motionless for the best part of half an hour, reviewing the situation. Then he leaped up.

"I must get the authorities to aid me," he thought. "I should have done this before."

He walked along the docks until he came to a street leading to the nearest police station. He now realized that he was hungry, but resolved to postpone eating until he had put the authorities on the track of the evildoers.

As he was turning a corner he almost ran into a colored man going in the opposite direction. The colored man stared at him, then let out a wild cry of delight.

"Massah Dick, or is I dreamin'?"

"Aleck, by all that's wonderful! Where did you come from?"

"From de yacht, ob course, Massah Dick. But—but—dis knocks dis niggah, suah! I dun fink yo' was on dat udder ship."

"I was on it, but I escaped yesterday, while the schooner lay in the river yonder."

"An' where am Tom and Sam, sah?"

"That I don't know. They left the vessel with me, but we

became separated in the water."

"Perhaps da dun been cotched ag'in," and Pop's face took on a sober look.

"That is what I am afraid of."

"Didn't see nuffin ob 'em nowhere?"

"No. I was hit by a lighter and knocked senseless."

"Whar's dat dar *Peacock*?"

"Gone, too."

"Wot you spects to do?"

"I was going to inform the authorities. We must find Tom and Sam."

"Dat's right, sah."

"Where is the *Swallow*?"

"Tied up jest below heah, sah. Dat dar Luke Peterson is a-sailin' ob her wid me."

"Good. Perhaps he can help us in the search. He knows these waters well, so he told me."

Together the pair made their way to the police station, where they told their stories to the officer in charge.

An alarm was at once sent out, and the river police were set to work to learn what had become of the *Peacock* and her crew.

But all this took time, and it was past noon when word came in that the schooner had been seen moving up Lake St. Clair on the afternoon of the day before.

Then word was telegraphed to Port Huron to stop the craft, and on his own responsibility Dick offered a reward of one hundred dollars for the capture of ship and master.

But all this came too late. Losing no time, Captain Langless had had his craft towed to a point fifteen miles beyond Port Huron, and had then let the tug go, and steered a course known only to those on board.

The tug did not return to Port Huron until the next day, and its captain did not know how much the *Peacock* was wanted until twenty-four hours later. Thus the schooner obtained a free and clear start of thirty-six hours over those who were in pursuit.

"We are stumped," groaned Dick, when word came back from Port Huron that the *Peacock* had passed that point long before. "That schooner now has the whole of Lake Huron before her, and there is no telling where she will go. Perhaps the Baxters will land in Canada."

"I don't think so," answered Luke Peterson. "American vessels coming in-shore are closely watched, you know, on account of the smuggling that is carried on."

"Then the smugglers between the United States and Canada are still at work."

"Indeed they are, more so than the average American has any idea of. I used to be in the customs service, and I know."

"Where do you suppose Captain Langless will go to?"

"Ah, that's a question, Rover. The lake is over two hundred miles long, and I've heard tell that there are over twenty-five hundred islands, large and small. That's a pretty good place for a ship to hide in, eh?"

"And you reckon the *Peacock* will go into hiding?"

"More than likely, while these Baxters carry out their little game— that is, providing your brothers are on board—and I fancy they are. I can tell ye, I fancy they are a tough crowd all around."

"Well, one comfort, the *Peacock* won't get very far anywhere along shore without being spotted, for the police have sent the news to all principal places."

"Well, that's a good plan. Now if we could only follow that schooner up—"

"Will you go with me in a hunt? I will willingly pay you for your services."

"I will. But we ought to have a steam tug instead of a yacht."

"I will charter one. I have already telegraphed to my father for the necessary funds," returned Dick, and he told the truth. The long telegram had gone an hour before. He had also sent word to Larry Colby, telling of the turn of affairs.

The telegram to Mr. Rover brought a characteristic reply, running as follows:

"I send you the money you want. Be careful and keep out of danger. Will come on by the first train."

The message to Larry Colby brought that student up to

Detroit on the first train from Sandusky.

"I know just the steam tug you want," said Larry, when the situation was explained. "It is rum by old Jack Parsons, who knows my father well. I know he will do all he can for you, if he is paid for his time."

Larry Colby undertook to hunt up the tug, which was named the *Rocket*, and found her tied up at one of the city docks. He introduced Dick, and before the hour was out a bargain was struck with Jack Parsons which was satisfactory all around. Parsons knew Luke Peterson, and said he would be glad to have the lumberman along on the hunt.

"He knows this lake as well as I do, and between us we ought to find the *Peacock*, sooner or later," said Parsons. He had heard about the raft disaster on Lake Erie, and was pleased to be able to inform Peterson that his friend Bragin was safe. The tug, however, which had been towing the raft, was laid up in Buffalo for repairs.

At first Dick thought to remain in Detroit until his father's arrival, but then he realized that it would be best for one of them to remain on shore while the other went on the hunt on the lake.

"We will sail at once," he said to his companions, but this could not be, since Aleck had not yet provided all of the necessary provisions for the trip.

While the colored man was completing his arrangements a newsboy came to Dick with a note, running as follows:

"If you want news of the *Peacock*, and will promise not to harm me, come with the boy to the old grain elevator. The boy knows the place."

Dick read the note with interest, and then showed it to Peterson.

"Perhaps it's a trap," said the lumberman. "I wouldn't go alone, if I were you."

"I will go," answered Dick, "but I wish you would follow me up on the quiet," and so it was arranged.

When Dick reached the place mentioned he found it practically deserted.

"Who gave you that note?" he asked of the newsboy.

"A man. Here he comes, now."

The newcomer proved to be a lame man, who had in former years been a sailor. He lived in a shanty behind the grain elevator, and he came to Dick with difficulty.

"Come into my shanty and I'll tell you what I know," said the lame man. "I'll not hurt you, so don't be afraid," and he hobbled off again.

Waving his hand to Peterson, who was in the distance, Dick followed the lame man and sat down on a bench in front of the shanty, the odd individual seating himself on a stool opposite.

"Want to find Captain Gus Langless, eh?" said the lame man, closing one eye suggestively.

"Yes."

"I read of the case in the papers. He's a bad un, eh?"

"What do you know of the case?" demanded Dick

impatiently. He realized that he had a decidedly queer individual with whom to deal.

"Know everything; yes, sir, everything. Jock Pelly don't keep his ears open for nothing, not me. An' I said to myself when I read the papers, 'Jock, you've learned something of value —you must sell the news,' says I to myself."

"But what do you know?"

"Gettin' to that, sir; gettin' there fast, too. Did you offer a reward of a hundred dollars?"

"Yes."

"Who's going to pay that amount? It's a pile of money, a hundred dollars is."

"It will be paid, you can be easy on that point."

"Well, supposin' a man is lame and can't go after those rascals? What does he git for puttin' somebody on the track?"

"If you put me on the right track, I'll give you fifty dollars."

"Dead certain?"

"Yes. Now where has the *Peacock* gone to?"

"Needle Point Island," was the abrupt answer. "Go there, an' you'll find the *Peacock* and her crew, sure."

CHAPTER XVI

OFF FOR NEEDLE POINT ISLAND

"Needle Point Island?" repeated Dick.

"Exactly, sir—Needle Point Island. Most of the lake pilots know it."

"How far is it from here?"

"About sixty miles."

"And how do you know the *Peacock* has gone there?"

"Overheard Captain Langless talking about it, yes, sir—overheard him talking to a man named Baxter and a man named Grimsby—he as used to be a smuggler. Langless used to be in with Grimsby, although few know o' that. They talked a lot, but that wouldn't interest you. But the fact that they are goin' to Needle Point Island interests you, eh?"

"When did you hear this talk?"

"The morning you escaped from the schooner, accordin' to the newspaper."

"Where did you hear it?"

"Up on the other side of the elevator. The men came out of one o' the saloons to talk it over."

A long conversation followed, and Dick became more than half convinced that what Jock Pelly had to relate was true.

The man described the Baxters clearly, showing that he had really seen the pair, and also described Captain Langless' appearance on the morning in question.

"I will follow up this clew," Dick said, when ready to depart.

Jock Pelly caught the youth by the arm.

"Hold on!"

"What do you want now?"

"My reward. Don't I get that fifty dollars?"

"You do, if I catch the captain and his schooner."

"That aint fair—I ought to have the money now."

"I must prove what you have told me first You may be all wrong in your suppositions."

Jock Pelly's face fell.

"'Taint fair—I ought to have the money now. Maybe you won't ever come back."

"Don't alarm yourself, my man. If the information is of real value, you'll get paid for it. Here is something on account."

Dick slipped a five-dollar bill into the old man's hand, at

which Jock Pelly's face relaxed. A few minutes later the elder Rover had joined Luke Peterson and was telling the lumberman what he had heard.

"Needle Point Island!" exclaimed Peterson. "Yes, I know the spot Years ago it was a great hanging-out place for smugglers. But our government cleaned out the nest."

"Then it is likely that this man told the truth?"

"I don't know as Captain Langless could find a better hiding place. The island is in the shape of a five-leaf clover, and the bays are all surrounded with tall trees and bushes, so that a vessel could be hidden there without half trying. Besides that, the island is a rough one, full of caves and openings, and that would just suit a crowd holding those boys prisoners."

When the pair reached the *Rocket* a consultation was held, and it was decided to start for Needle Point Island on the following morning. Jack Parsons said it would take from five to six hours to reach the locality.

Now that Dick had received what he thought was definite information, he was anxious to go to the island that had been mentioned, consequently the night proved a long and sleepless one to him. He awaited further news from his father, but none came.

But information did come which disturbed him not a little. He was speaking to Larry before retiring, and from one thing to another the conversation drifted around to Mrs. Stanhope, the widow who lived near Putnam Hall, and her pretty daughter Dora. As old readers know Dick was tremendously interested in pretty Dora, and had done much to keep her from harm.

Arthur M. Winfield

"Before I came on, I heard that the Stanhopes had started on a trip for the lakes," said Larry. "They left Cedarville secretly, and I got the news quite by accident from Frank Harrington, who happened to see them off."

"I knew they were going, sooner or later," replied Dick. "Mrs. Stanhope was rather ill, as you know, and needed a change of some sort."

"I was wondering if she didn't want to get out of the way of Josiah Crabtree, who is just out of prison," continued Larry. "Oh, but wasn't he a slick one for getting around the widow—when he learned she was holding all that money in trust for Dora."

"He's something of a hypnotist, Larry—that is why Dora fears him. She is afraid he will hypnotize her mother into doing something she will be sorry for afterward."

"Do you really suppose he has so much influence as that?"

"He has when Mrs. Stanhope is not feeling well. The stronger she is, the less he seems to affect her. By the way, have you heard from old Crabtree since he was let out of jail?"

"Yes; some of us boys met him at Ithaca one Saturday. We started to have a little fun with him, asking him why he didn't come back to the Hall and ask Captain Putnam for another position, and how he liked live crabs in his bed. But he flew in a rage and threatened to have us all arrested if we didn't clear out, so we had to drop it. But I'll tell you one thing, Dick; I'll wager Crabtree's up to no good."

"Oh! he might possibly turn over a new leaf."

"Not he; it isn't in him. He was always a sneak, like Baxter, only a bit more high-toned, outwardly."

"I am anxious to know if he is aware where the Stanhopes have gone to?"

"I think he could find out if he tried hard. They made a mistake that they didn't go traveling before he got out of jail."

"They couldn't go, on account of Mrs. Stanhope's health. She had a relapse just about the time Crabtree's term was up. But he had better not bother them again, or—"

"Or what, Dick? Will you get after him again?"

"I will if I can, and I'll send him to jail for the rest of his life."

The *Rocket* was to sail at six in the morning, and long before that time Dick and Larry, with the others, were on board. Jack Parsons reached the tug at the last moment, having had some private business which required his attention.

The day was fair, with a stiff breeze blowing, which was good for the *Peacock*, as Dick observed, if she was still sailing the waters of the lake.

Jack Parsons knew Needle Point Island as well as did Luke Peterson, and the former said he had stopped at the place only a few months before.

"I thought it was deserted," he said. "The old cave the smugglers used to use was tumbled in and overgrown with brush."

The run to Port Huron occurred without incident, and a little while later the *Rocket* was steaming merrily over the clear waters of Lake Huron.

Had it not been for his anxiety concerning his two brothers, Dick would have enjoyed the scene very much. The *Rocket* was a fine tug, and cut the water like a thing of life. She carried a crew of five, all young and active fellows. This made the party eight, all told, and as Dick and his friends were armed and the tug boasted of several pistols, a gun, and a small cannon, those on board felt themselves able to cope with the enemy, no matter what occurred.

"We can't get there any too soon for me," said Dick to Luke Peterson. "There is no telling how cruelly Sam and Tom are being treated, now that they made the attempt to run away."

"I hope your father doesn't give the rascals any money before we have a chance to catch them," returned the lumberman.

"I think he will wait to hear from me, after he reads the letter I left for him at Detroit. He is as down on the Baxters as I am,"

"When we come in sight of the island we'll have to move with caution," went on the lumberman. "If we don't, Captain Langless may lay low and give us the slip in the dark."

"Are there any other islands close to Needle Point?"

"A dozen of them, and some with just as good hiding places, too. That's why the smugglers used to hang out in that locality. They are ideal places for smugglers' caves and the like, I can tell ye that," and Luke Peterson nodded his head sagaciously.

At noon Parsons announced that they were within three miles of Needle Point Island. Dinner was ready, but it must be confessed that Dick was almost too excited to eat. Half a dozen vessels had thus far been sighted, but not one which looked like the *Peacock*.

He was finishing up a hasty repast when a cry came from the deck.

"Needle Point Island is in sight!" announced the lookout, and a moment later he added: "A schooner bearing away to the bay on the east end!"

"It must be the *Peacock*!" ejaculated Dick, and rushed to the deck to learn the truth.

Arthur M. Winfield

CHAPTER XVII

A CAVE AND A SNAKE

"Now we are in for it, Sam. They won't give us a second chance to escape."

A groan was the answer, coming from out of the darkness of the hold of the *Peacock*. Sam was too much stunned and bruised to reply to the words from his brother.

The two boys had been hustled on board of the schooner with scant ceremony, and now they found themselves bound and handcuffed, so that it was next to impossible for either of them to move. Hour after hour had passed, yet nobody had come near them.

"I reckon they are going to starve us to death for what we did," went on Tom, after a long pause.

"If only I had a drink of water," came at last from his younger brother. "My mouth is as dry as a chip, and I seem to have a regular fever."

"Make the best of it, Sam," returned Tom soothingly. "This state of things can't last forever. If they—Oh!"

The schooner had suddenly tacked in the strong wind, and

The Rover Boys on the Great Lakes   133

the bowling over of the empty craft had caused Tom to take a long roll. He struck up against his brother, and the pair went sliding to the end of the hold, to hit a jug of water which had been left there in the darkness.

"Hurrah, some water!" cried Tom, as some of the fluid splashed over his hand. But, alas! how were they to get at what was left of the contents of the jug, with their hands tied behind them?

But time was no object, and at last they solved the problem. At first Tom backed up to the jug and held it, though clumsily, for Sam to drink, and then the youngest Rover did the same for his brother. The water was warm and somewhat stale, yet both could remember nothing which had ever tasted sweeter to them. They drank about half of what the jug contained, then set the rest carefully away for future use.

The *Peacock* was bowling along at a speed of seven or eight knots an hour, and the creaking of the blocks attested the fact that Captain Langless was making every effort to reach his destination as soon as possible.

Once the boys heard somebody at the forward hatchway, and presently the hatch was lifted for a few inches.

"Hope you are enjoying yourselves down there," came in the sarcastic tones of Dan Baxter. To this they made no answer, and the hatch was closed as quickly as it had been opened.

"The brute," muttered Tom. "I'd give a good deal to be able to punch his nose!"

"He evidently thinks himself on top to stay," came from Sam, who had propped himself up against an empty cask. "Oh, if only we knew what had become of Dick!" he went on.

"Dick must have escaped. I don't see how it could be otherwise."

"But if he did, why didn't he notify the authorities?"

"The *Peacock* must have given the river police the slip; that's the only answer I can make, Sam."

"But they could have telegraphed to different points."

"Well, I can't make it out, and we'll have to take what comes."

"Where do you suppose we are bound?"

"I haven't the least idea."

Hour after hour went by, and still nobody came to them. It did, indeed, look as if they were to be starved to death. But just as Sam was almost fainting for the want of food, the door to the cabin passageway was flung open, and Captain Langless appeared with a lantern, followed by Arnold Baxter, who carried a tray containing a plate of bread and two bowls of beef stew.

"Hungry, I'll wager," said the captain laconically. All the pleasantness he had previously exhibited had vanished.

"You ought to be ashamed of yourselves to let us starve so long," replied Tom, who never hesitated to speak his mind.

"Hi! don't talk that way, or you shall have nothing," cried Arnold Baxter. "We are masters, and you must understand it so."

The captain set down the lantern and released the right hand of each of the prisoners. Then the tray was set upon an upturned box, and they were told to eat what they wanted, the captain and Arnold Baxter sitting down to watch them.

There was no use to "stand upon then dignity," as Tom afterward expressed it, so they fell to without protest, and it must be confessed that the stew was just what their stomachs, in that weakened state, needed. It did not take long to get away with the larger portion of the bread and all of what the bowls contained.

"You can thank your stars that you got meal," said Arnold Baxter. "You don't deserve it."

"According to you, I suppose we don't deserve anything but abuse," replied Tom. "But, never mind, Arnold Baxter; remember the old saying, 'He laughs best who laughs last.'"

"I'm not here to listen to your back talk," growled Arnold Baxter. "Come, captain, let us be going," and he arose.

"You've brought this treatment on yourselves," said the captain, with a shrewd look into the boys' faces. "I was of a mind to treat you kindly before. You know that."

"Come," insisted Arnold Baxter, and caught the captain by the arm. "Don't waste words on them. There will be time enough to talk when we reach the island." And then the two walked off, closing and locking the passageway door after them.

"The island?" repeated Sam. "Then they intend to take us to some lonely island, Tom!"

"I wouldn't be surprised. I've noticed by the shafts of light coming through the cracks overhead that we are sailing northward. We must be in Lake Huron by this time."

"One satisfaction, they left our right hands free," continued the youngest Rover. "And I must say that stew just touched the spot."

Again the hours drifted slowly by. The boys had really lost all track of time. They dozed off and did not awaken until some time later. Whether they had slept through a night or not they did not know.

Presently they heard the sails being lowered and an anchor go overboard. Then a boat put off from the *Peacock*, and for a while all became silent.

"We must be close to some landing," was Tom's comment. "Perhaps it's the island old Baxter mentioned."

Another half hour slipped by. Then the door to the cabin was opened, and both Baxters, Captain Langless, and the mate of the schooner appeared.

"Get up," ordered the captain, and when they arose he saw to it that their lower limbs were released, but that their hands were bound more tightly behind them than ever.

"We are going ashore," said Arnold Baxter, "Remember we want no treachery nor any attempt to run away. If you try either, somebody will get shot."

With this caution they were marched into the cabin and then on deck. At first the strong light blinded them, but soon they became accustomed to this, and made out a small bay just ahead, surrounded by cedar trees and various bushes. Back of the trees was a hill, and off to the southward a rocky elevation ending in a needle-like point. It was this elevation which gave to the island the name of Needle Point. By the Indians of days gone by the island was called Arrow Head.

A rowboat was in waiting beside the *Peacock*, and into this the prisoners were placed. The captain of the schooner and the Baxters also went along, and soon the rowboat had passed over the waters of the little bay and grounded on a bit of shelving beach.

"Now we'll go ashore," said Captain Langless, and glad enough for the change, Tom and Sam leaped upon the beach. The others followed, and tying up the boat, the master of the *Peacock* led the way through the trees and brush to the hill previously mentioned. Here there was a slight path, winding in and out among a series of rocks.

"Where are you going to take us?" said Tom.

"You'll find out soon enough," returned Arnold Baxter. "March."

"Supposing I refuse?"

"We'll knock you down and drag you along," put in Dan Baxter, anxious to say something.

"You had better come along quietly," said Captain Langless. "To kick will only make you worse off."

The march was resumed, and now they dove straight into the interior of the island, which was about a mile and a half long and half as wide. At some points the path was choked with weeds and trailing vines, and they progressed with difficulty.

It must be admitted that Tom and Sam were very uneasy. They had felt that the authorities might follow the *Peacock*, but how would anybody ever discover them in such a lonely place as this? But there was no help for it, and on they went until Captain Langless called a sudden halt.

They had gained a cliff running out from one end of the hill. The rocks arose in a sheer wall, thirty or more feet in height. At the base were a spring and a small pool of water. To the left of the spring was a cave-like opening, partly choked with brushwood.

"Here we are," said the captain. "Watch them."

He moved toward the opening and soon had a portion of the brushwood torn aside. Then he lit a lantern he had brought along and disappeared into the opening.

He had scarcely passed from view when he let out a yell of fright.

"A snake! Look out for him!"

The words just reached the ears of Sam and Tom when the reptile appeared. He was all of five feet long and as thick as a man's wrist.

"A snake!" screamed Dan Baxter, and took to his heels without waiting to see what the creature might do.

Arnold Baxter was less frightened, and snatching a pistol from his pocket, he took hasty aim and fired. But his aim was poor, and the bullet flew wide of its mark.

The snake was a dangerous one, and very much shot, and came straight for Tom and Sam. An instant later the savage reptile was coiling itself around the youngest Rover's left leg!

CHAPTER XVIII

COFFEE FOR THREE

The situation was one which demanded instant action.

The snake was a dangerous one, and very much aroused, and it might at any instant do Sam great harm.

The poor boy was speechless and motionless, for the reptile had caught his eye and held him as by a spell.

It was Tom who acted. Heedless of the danger, he leaped forward and aimed a kick at the snake's head.

The reptile was caught fairly and squarely, and the head went down with an angry hiss. Then Tom stepped upon it, but the snake squirmed loose and uttered another hiss, louder than before.

"Take him off! Take him off!" screamed Sam, now recovering his voice. "Don't let him bite me."

He would have caught the snake himself, and so would Tom, but the hands of both were still tied behind them.

By this time Captain Langless emerged from the cave, pulling out a pistol as he did so.

Arnold Baxter had not offered to fire a second shot. Now, he was out of danger himself, he did not seem to care what became of the Rovers.

Crack! crack! It was the captain's weapon which spoke up, and the two shots, fired in rapid succession, did their work thoroughly. The first took the snake in the neck and the second in the head, and in a twinkle the long, slippery body unwound itself from Sam's leg and began to turn and twist on the ground.

"Good for you!" gasped Sam, when able to speak again. "Ugh! what an ugly thing!" And he retreated to the opposite side of the pool, along with Tom.

"He was a nasty one," replied Captain Langless, as he coolly proceeded to reload his pistol. "I might have killed him in the cave, only the light was bad."

"Is he—he dead?" came from behind some rocks, and Dan showed a white face and trembling form.

"Yes, he's dead," answered Arnold Baxter. "I came pretty close to hitting him," he went on, bound to say something for himself.

"I—I thought there was a whole nest of them," continued Dan. "If I had known there was only one, I would have stood my ground."

"Of course—you always were brave," answered Tom sarcastically.

"See here, Tom Rover, I don't want any of your back talk," howled the bully, his face turning red.

"Come, don't quarrel now," said Captain Langless, so

sternly that Dan subsided on the instant. "The question is, are there any more snakes in that cave?"

"Send Dan in to investigate," suggested Sam, with just the faintest touch of his old-time light-heartedness.

"Me?" ejaculated the individual mentioned. "Not me! I wouldn't go in there for a million dollars!"

"Perhaps we had better find some other cave," said Arnold Baxter. "You said there were several around here."

"This is as good as any," answered Captain Langless. "If you are afraid, I'll go in myself," and turning, he disappeared once more into the opening, lantern in one hand and pistol in the other.

He was gone the best part of quarter of an hour, and came back covered with dust and dirt.

"The old spot is pretty well choked up with rubbish," he said. "But there isn't a sign of another snake around, nor of any wild beasts. Come," and he motioned Sam and Tom to follow him.

"I don't think it fair that you should leave us helpless," said Tom. "At least untie our hands and let us each get a good stick."

"So you can fight us, eh?" cried Arnold Baxter. "We are not such fools."

"You have your pistols," put in Sam. "And what could we do on a lonely island and without a boat?"

"The lads are right—it's not fair to leave them helpless when there may be other danger at hand," interposed the captain.

Arthur M. Winfield

"If I unloosen you, will you promise not to run away?"

"The promise would not amount to anything!" sniffed Dan.

"We won't run away for the present," said Tom honestly. "But you can't expect me to remain a prisoner here—not if I can help myself."

The candor of the youth compelled Captain Langless to laugh, and, taking out a knife, he cut the ropes which bound the lads' hands.

"You won't need sticks, I am sure of it," he said. "Come, I will lead, and you"—nodding to the Baxters—"can bring up the rear."

No more was said, and in a minute more all were inside of the cave, which proved to be fifteen feet wide, about as high, and at least two hundred feet long. At the lower end were a turn and a narrow passageway leading to the darkness beyond. The ceiling was rough, and the lantern cast long, dancing shadows over it as they advanced. Sam could not help but shiver, and Tom looked unusually sober.

That the cave had once been used as a rendezvous of some sort was plainly evident. At the back was a rude fireplace, with a narrow slit in the rocks overhead, through which the smoke might ascend. Here were several half-burned logs of wood, and two tumble-down boxes which had evidently done duty as benches. On a stick stuck in a crack of the wall hung an old overcoat, now ready to fall apart from decay.

"Rather unwholesome, I admit," said the captain, with a glance at the others. "But a roaring fire in yonder chimney-place will soon alter things. And when I've had one of the men bring some blankets and stores from the *Peacock*, it will be fairly comfortable."

"Do you mean to keep us here?" demanded Tom.

"We do," answered Arnold Baxter. "And you can thank your stars that you have not been taken to a worse place."

"It's a jolly shame. Why don't you kill us off at once, and be done with it?"

"Because you are worth more to us alive than dead."

"We won't live long if you keep us here," put in Sam. "It's enough to give a fellow the ague."

"We will start a fire without delay," said the captain, and then, turning to Arnold Baxter, he continued: "Can you find the way back to the ship?"

"I think I can," returned the other. "Years ago I was used to tramping the gold regions of the West."

"Then you had better go and tell the mate to bring along that stuff I mentioned before I left. You can easily carry the stuff between you. I'll build the fire and, with the aid of your son, watch the two prisoners."

So it was arranged, although Arnold Baxter did not fancy the task of carrying stuff to be used for the Rovers' comfort. He left his pistol with Dan, who kept it in his hand, ready to shoot should Sam or Tom make the slightest movement toward getting away.

As Captain Langless had said, the fire made the cave far more comfortable, taking away the feeling of dampness and lighting up all the nooks and corners. From a distance the boys heard a faint falling of water, and were told that it came from a spring hidden at the rear passageway.

Arthur M. Winfield

It was a good hour before Arnold Baxter returned, lugging a fair-sized bundle, and followed by the mate of the *Peacock* with an even greater load. They had several blankets and a basket of provisions, and likewise a few cooking utensils.

"Evidently out for a stay," muttered Tom, as he looked at the things.

"They are for your use," was Captain Langless' grim reply. "After this I reckon you'll cook for yourselves."

"Do you expect us to remain in this cave night and day?"

"You'll remain whenever things look suspicious outside."

"Then you'll let us go out otherwise?"

"If you behave yourselves."

It was not long before Tom and Sam were left in the cave alone. The mate of the schooner was placed at the entrance on guard, armed with the captain's own pistol. Then Captain Langless and the Baxters withdrew, talking earnestly. Tom and Sam could not catch the drift of the conversation, although they heard the words "by mail" and "we must get the cash" used several times.

"They are bound to make money out of this affair, if they can," remarked Tom, when he and Sam were alone once more.

"I've a good mind to knock that mate down and take the pistol from him," said Sam.

"And get shot for your pains? Besides, if we took away the pistol and put him out of the fight, what next? We haven't any boat to get away in."

"Yes, but I don't intend to remain here a prisoner forever."

"No more do I, but we can do nothing just now. Let us see what kind of a meal we can make out of the provisions brought to us."

The prospect of a meal brightened up both lads, and they set to work with a will, and soon had coffee made. There were bread and butter and some canned beef and beans, and they ate heartily.

The mate sniffed the coffee, and remarked that it seemed good.

"Have a cup," said Tom cheerily.

"No funny work, boy," and Cadmus looked at the boys suspiciously. "No break like that you tried on me before."

"No, I won't run, honor bright," answered Tom, and then the mate took the coffee and drank it with much satisfaction.

As he set down the cup he gazed fixedly at both Tom and Sam for several seconds. Then he drew himself up as if he had come to some mental decision.

"I've got a plan to propose," he said slowly. "Do you want to listen or not?"

"What sort of a plan?" asked both.

"A plan to get you out of the clutches of Captain Langless and those Baxters," was the answer, which filled Tom and Sam with deep and sudden interest.

146   Arthur M. Winfield

CHAPTER XIX

AN ASTONISHING DISCOVERY

"Are you willing to help us to get away?" cried Sam.

"Under certain circumstances I am," replied the mate of the schooner. "Captain Langless didn't treat me square after you got away from me, and Andy Cadmus aint the tar to forget such a thing in a hurry."

"What are your conditions?" asked Tom.

"The conditions are two in number. In the first place, if I help you, will you promise, in case the plan falls through, that you will not tell Captain Langless what I did, but let him believe that you got away on your own hook?"

"We'll promise that readily enough," answered Tom, and Sam nodded.

"In the second place, if I get you away from them and see you to a place of safety, will you promise to help clear me in case those others are brought to trial?"

"We will," came from both.

"Is that all you want?" continued Tom.

"Almost. But there is one other condition I forgot to mention."

"I know what that is," said Sam. "It's money."

"Correct, lad. It's money. I'm a poor man, and what little I have is on board the *Peacock*. Your father is rich. If I help you, it ought to be worth something to him."

"How much?" asked Tom cautiously.

"Well, say a couple of hundred dollars. I won't ask for too much."

"You shall have the money," answered Tom quickly, "on condition you will aid us in bringing the Baxters to justice."

"Then it's a bargain," and Andy Cadmus drew another long breath. "Now for the details of our plan."

The mate sat down on a stone at the mouth of the cave and filled a pipe with tobacco, lit it, and fell to smoking thoughtfully.

"The details ought to be simple enough," said Tom. "When you go back to the *Peacock* you can take one of the small boats, stock her with provisions, and then go off in her. Then we can join you."

"It won't work, unless you have a fight with whoever happens to be on guard here—and that may mean trouble for you. I have a better scheme."

"What's that?"

"To-night, when I'm on watch, I'll stock one of the small boats and take her to shore and hide her in the bushes.

Arthur M. Winfield

Then, when I'm on guard again here, we can all cut sticks and take to the little boat."

"Will you carry out the plan to-night?" asked Sam.

"If I can."

So it was arranged, and then the three talked over the details. Cadmus said it was a good tern miles to the nearest point of the mainland, but that he was certain he could steer almost a straight course thither.

A couple of hours later one of the sailors from the *Peacock* came up, all out of breath, and told the mate to return to the schooner with all speed.

"The cap'n wants ye," he said, but would not explain why.

"What's the trouble?" asked Tom, when the sailor was on guard, but the newcomer refused to talk about the affair further than to say that he guessed Cadmus would not be back to do additional sentinel duty.

"If that's the case, our plan to escape is knocked in the head," whispered Sam, as he and Tom withdrew to the fire. "Was ever there luck before!"

"I move we try to escape without further delay," returned Tom. He was in a reckless mood.

"Shall we tackle the guard?"

"Let us try a bit of strategy," and then the pair held a whispered consultation lasting several minutes.

Returning to the mouth of the cave Tom took up his position at one side and Sam on the other. Talking of things in general at first, they gradually put the sailor in good humor, and then turned on the subject of snakes.

"That was a bad snake we killed," said Tom. "I sincerely hope there are no more around the cave."

"Snakes are ugly things," said the sailor, shaking his head vigorously.

"Ever see a sea serpent?" questioned Sam.

"No. I reckon there aint none on the lakes, like there are in the ocean. I've got a cousin sails the Pacific. He's seen serpents lots o' times—on the shores of them far-off islands."

"I don't believe a sea serpent is half as bad as a land snake," continued Sam. "Why, that snake was enough to give a fellow the jim-jams, he was so long and slimy, and had such a bad look in his blazing eyes. He wound right around my leg and was just going to strike, when—My gracious! look at that snake behind you!"

Worked up over what Sam was relating, and totally unconscious of the trick being played upon him, the sailor leaped up and turned around. As he did this, Tom came up behind him swiftly and pinioned his arms to his side. Then Sam rushed in and caught hold of the gun.

"Hi, stop!" roared the sailor. "Let go! This aint fair nohow!"

"Keep still, if you don't want to be shot," answered Tom. And he continued to hold the fellow, while Sam gave the gun a dexterous twist and got it loose. Then the youngest Rover aimed the weapon at the sailor's head.

"Up with your hands," he said, as coolly as he could, although his heart was pumping like mad.

Arthur M. Winfield

Tom released his hold, and fearful of being shot, the sailor raised his hands as commanded. Then Tom picked up the ropes still lying near and proceeded to bind the sailor's legs together.

The fellow wished to yell for help, but Tom's stern glance kept him silent.

"Now what shall we do with him?" asked Sam.

"Carry him into the cave," replied his brother. "Somebody else from the schooner is bound to come, sooner or later, and release him."

"I don't want to go in with them snakes," said the tar. "Leave me out here."

"There are no more snakes in there," said Tom. "We'll place you close to the fire, so you'll be comfortable and in no danger of either snakes or wild beasts."

With this the boys lugged the sailor into the cave. They wasted no time, for there was no telling when some others of their enemies might put in an appearance.

"Now which way?" asked Sam, when the pair were again outside. "I wonder how big this island is?"

"Big enough for us to hide on, I imagine, Sam. Let us go in the opposite direction to which we came."

They skirted the cliff and then plunged into the woods beyond. As they progressed Tom cautioned his brother to keep to the rocks as much as possible, in order that the trail might be hidden.

It was still hot, and before long the exertion of climbing the rocks and picking their way through the dense underbrush told upon them. Coming to the top of a small hill, they halted.

"Let us climb into yonder tree and rest," said Sam. "Perhaps we can see the *Peacock* from that point."

This seemed a good idea, and they moved to the very top of the tallest tree to be found.

A grand view lay spread before their gaze. Close upon every side was the thickly wooded island, sloping gradually down to the lake, and beyond, as far as eye could reach, was the rolling water, sparkling brightly in the sunlight. To the northward Tom discovered a bit of greenery, which he rightly took for another island.

But what interested them most was the appearance of a ship riding at anchor to the westward, in one of the several bays previously mentioned. It was a sailing vessel of fair size, carrying a single mast.

"That's not the *Peacock*!" ejaculated Sam.

"You're right!" cried Tom. "She's a stranger. Hurrah! Perhaps Dick has followed us up, after all!"

"Anyway, we ought to find friends on that ship, Tom. Let us get to her as soon as possible."

"I'm willing. But I must rest a bit, I'm so dead tired."

"I wish we could get those on the strange ship to make the Baxters and Captain Langless prisoners."

"Perhaps we can. But it will be a good deal to get out of the clutches of the enemy, even if we can't do any more."

Feeling much elated over the discovery of the strange vessel, the boys rested for quarter of an hour, and then, descending to the ground, struck out rapidly once more through the woods and underbrush. As they proceeded Tom carried his pistol in his hand, in case some wild animal might start up in their path, but nothing of the sort came to view.

As they came closer to the shore they found that the ground was wet and boggy, and they had to pick their way with care. Once Sam went into the soil up to his ankles, and dragged himself out only with great difficulty. Then they made a detour, coming out on the beach some distance below where the strange ship was anchored.

Halting behind a convenient bush, they surveyed the ship with interest. On the deck they discovered a man and a lady. The lady was sitting in an easy-chair, and the man stood by, leaning on a railing. Both were talking earnestly.

"Well I never!" came from Tom. "Sam, do you recognize those two people?"

"I do," was the answer. "Josiah Crabtree and Mrs. Stanhope! How in the world did they get here?"

CHAPTER XX

JOSIAH CRABTREE'S GAME

For the moment the boys were practically dumfounded. Josiah Crabtree and Mrs. Stanhope in this out-of-the-way place? What could it mean?

"They are arguing about something," said Tom, after a long pause. "Hear how earnestly old Crabtree is talking to her?"

"I wonder if Dora is with them."

"I don't see anything of her."

"What shall we do?"

"I don't know—excepting to remain hidden until we learn how the land lays."

The boys considered the situation for a while, and then, by turning back into the woods, managed to come up at a point still closer to the ship, which rested at anchor close to the trunk of a fallen tree.

Here they could hear the most of what was being said, and could also obtain a fair look at the side of Mrs. Stanhope's face. Josiah Crabtree's back was turned to them. They noticed that Mrs. Stanhope's face wore a peculiar, drawn expression, like that of one who is walking in his sleep.

"I'll wager he's been hypnotizing her again," whispered Tom. "Oh, what a rascal he is! Just as bad as the Baxters, every bit!"

"I do not, cannot, understand it all," the lady was saying. "I thought Dora and I were to take this trip alone."

"It will all be clear to you in a few days, Pet," returned the ex-school-teacher soothingly. He had lately gotten to calling the lady "Pet," although that was not her real name.

"Where is my child now? I do not wish to remain on board without her."

"She will be back soon; do not worry."

"I thought the trip would do me much good," continued the lady, with a deep sigh. "But I am more feeble than ever, and I cannot think as clearly as I would wish."

"It may be that this lake air is too strong for you, Pet. To-morrow we will take a run ashore. The village of Nestwood is close at hand, and I dare say I can find very good accommodations for you there."

"Will Dora be with me?"

"Perhaps."

"I do not wish to go ashore without her. She always said we would be safe on the boat."

"And you are safe."

"But she didn't want me to—that is, she didn't expect you to be along."

"She has changed her mind about that, Pet. I had a long talk with her and proved to her that she had been mistaken in me, and that I was not as black as painted."

"But they put you in jail."

"All a mistake, as I told you before. It was the work of those rascally Rover boys."

"I like that," muttered Tom. "Isn't he a peach, though, for smoothing matters over?"

"He has hypnotized her, beyond a doubt," returned Sam. "She would never believe him otherwise."

"And what did Dora say?" went on Mrs. Stanhope, after a pause, during which Josiah Crabtree took a turn up and down the deck.

"She is perfectly willing that we should marry, but under one condition."

"And what is that?"

"I hardly dare to tell you—it is so peculiar. She doesn't wish to be present at the ceremony."

"Not present?"

"No. She says it would not be right. That she very foolishly made a vow never to be present should you marry again, and that she must keep that vow. She feels her position keenly, but she won't break her vow."

Such a statement would have aroused any ordinary woman, but Mrs. Stanhope appeared to be completely in Josiah Crabtree's power, and all she did now was to draw a long sigh and then wipe away a tear which stole down her pallid face.

"I do not think it right that I should marry without Dora being present."

"Pooh! If the girl wishes to remain away, let her do so. She will soon come to her senses and be glad of the way matters have turned."

"You do not know Dora. She is very—very headstrong at times."

"Yes, I do know her, Pet. She is headstrong, and greatly influenced by those Rover boys—especially by Dick Rover, who seems to be—ahem— somewhat smitten with her."

"Dick always impressed me as being a good youth."

"Good? He is anything but that. Why, if it wasn't for the Rovers, I would now have the finest boarding school for boys on Cayuga Lake. They spoiled all the plans I ever made. But they shall do so no longer. They cross my path again at their peril!"

"The tragic old fraud!" whispered Tom. "I've a good mind to face him just where he stands."

"Go slow! We dun't know who is on board of that ship."

"Evidently friends to Crabtree, or they wouldn't let him hypnotize Dora's mother."

"Where can Dora be?"

"That remains to be found out."

"I wonder where that ship hails from?"

"One of the lake towns. She is an old vessel. There is the name—*Wellington*. That sounds as if she might be a Canadian."

"Perhaps Crabtree got both of them into Canada and then cast Dora adrift."

There was now a stir on the ship, and a fat old sailor came on deck.

"How long you say we stay in dees island, hey?" he asked, in a strong French-Canadian accent.

"We will sail as soon as the sun goes down," answered Josiah Crabtree.

"I no lak to stay here," went on the sailor, "You no pay for to stay here."

"I will pay you for your full time," answered the ex-school-teacher smoothly. "Do not worry on that account."

"You go on de land, hey?"

"I think not. We shall set sail for Nestwood, as I told you before."

"Is Dora at Nestwood?" questioned Mrs. Stanhope.

"I expect to meet her there. But she may not show up until after the wedding, my dear."

"It is very, very strange," and Mrs. Stanhope sighed again.

The fat old sailor now went below again, and after a few words more with Mrs. Stanhope Josiah Crabtree followed.

"Now is our chance!" whispered Tom. "You stay here and I'll try to have a talk with Mrs. Stanhope in secret."

So speaking, Tom crawled out upon the fallen tree trunk until he could reach a rope hanging over the *Wellington's* side. Then he drew himself up silently.

"Oh!" cried Mrs. Stanhope, on catching sight of him. "Is it really you, Tom Rover?"

"Hush, Mrs. Stanhope! not so loud," he replied hastily. "I don't want to let Josiah Crabtree know I am here."

"But where did you come from?"

"From the island. It's a long story. I am here with Sam."

"It is very strange. But many things of late have been strange."

"May I ask how you happen to be here?"

"That, too, is a long story. I was to take a trip with Dora, for the benefit of my health. But, on the way to the lakes Dora disappeared and Mr. Crabtree turned up in her place—and he has been with me ever since."

"He wants to marry you, doesn't he?"

"Yes, he has always wished that, as you know."

"I wouldn't do it. He is after your money, and that is all. He is a fraud, and everybody knows it."

Mrs. Stanhope passed her hand over her brow. Tom's blunt words did much to counteract Josiah Crabtree's strange influence over her.

"Your words impress me deeply," she faltered. "Dora talks that way, too. But—but—Mr. Crabtree, when he is with me, makes me think so differently." She tried to get up, then sank back in her seat. "And I am so weak physically!"

"Don't alarm yourself, Mrs. Stanhope. If you need a friend, I'll stand by you—and so will Sam."

"Where is Dick? You boys are always together."

"I don't know where he is at present. We were carried off by the Baxters, who are not far off."

"The Baxters! Oh, I am afraid of those people—more afraid than I ever was of Mr. Crabtree."

"They are certainly more daring, but no worse morally than Crabtree." Tom ran his hand through his curly hair in perplexity. "Who is aboard of this boat?"

"Mr. Crabtree and myself, two sailors, and one of the sailors' wives, who has been waiting on me."

"Not a very large crowd."

"Mr. Crabtree said he did not wish too many along."

"How long have you been here on the lake?"

"Several days. I did not wish to go, but, but—"

"He has an influence over you?"

"Yes, a strange influence I cannot understand. Oh, I am so wretched!" And the lady suddenly burst into tears.

"Don't, please don't!" said Tom, all sympathy at once. "It's Crabtree's work, and he shan't harm you. I'll see you safe back to Dora and home."

"Will you?" she demanded eagerly. "I do not wish to marry unless Dora is pleased. She said—"

Mrs. Stanhope got no further, for at that instant Josiah Crabtree reappeared on deck. His astonishment at seeing Tom can better be imagined than described.

CHAPTER XXI

TOM BRINGS ONE ENEMY TO TERMS

"Am I dreaming?" gasped the former school-teacher, when he could command his voice sufficiently to speak.

"You might better be dreaming, Josiah Crabtree," replied Tom, eying the man sharply. "This is a bad business you are engaged in."

"Where did you come from?"

"None of your business."

"Don't be impertinent, young man."

"Then don't try to pry into my private affairs."

"Have you been following this boat?" questioned Crabtree nervously.

"Never mind what I've been doing. I have found you out, and that appears to be a good job done."

"Found me out? What do you mean to insinuate by that?"

"I mean that you are up to no good; that's what I mean, Mr.

Arthur M. Winfield

Josiah Crabtree, A. M."

"You are very, very—"

"Don't try to abuse me, it won't work. I want to know what you propose to do with Mrs. Stanhope."

"That is my affair—or, rather, it is the affair of that lady and myself—and does not concern such a scamp as you."

"Oh, Josiah! I do not think Tom is a scamp," broke in Mrs. Stanhope, in a pleading voice.

"He is a scamp, and worse, Pet. Allow me to deal with him alone."

"So you thought to elope with Mrs. Stanhope," went on Tom sarcastically. "To elope without Dora being the wiser."

"Ha! what do you know of Dora!" ejaculated the man, starting back in alarm.

"I know a good deal."

"Has she—ahem! followed me?"

"Would that surprise you?"

"It is—er—very extraordinary." Crabtree cleared his throat. "I—that is—where is she now?" And he looked around.

"I told you I wasn't answering questions. But you had better take my advice and go slow, or you'll soon find yourself in jail again."

"You must have followed us in a boat. Where is your craft?"

"Another question which I am not answering. Do you surrender?"

"Surrender?"

"That is what I said."

"I—er—don't understand."

"The case is very simple. You ran off with Mrs. Stanhope, influencing her against her will to accompany you. Your game is to marry her so that you can get hold of the money she is holding in trust for Dora— "

"It is false!"

"It is the plain truth. Josiah Crabtree, you are a trickster of the first water, but if I can prevent your trickery I am going to do it." Tom turned to Mrs. Stanhope, who was now crying violently. "Won't you go below and let me have it out with this man?"

"Oh, I trust there will be no violence!" she sobbed.

"I shall teach this young upstart a lesson," fumed Josiah Crabtree. He saw that Tom's coming had greatly lessened his influence over the lady.

"Please go below, Mrs. Stanhope, and don't worry about me," said Tom.

"Yes, it will be best," added Crabtree, and then the lady disappeared down the companion way, walking slowly, for she felt weaker than ever, because of the excitement.

"Now, sir, we will come to an understanding," said the former teacher of Putnam Hall, as he faced Tom with a show of severe dignity.

"Very well, we will come to an understanding."

"You have followed me to here."

"Granted."

"You came in another boat with Dora."

"What if I did? Do you suppose I would come with her alone?" went on Tom, struck with a sudden idea.

"Do you mean to say you have—er—brought along any of the—ahem!— authorities?" And Josiah Crabtree glanced around nervously.

"I am not alone—nor is Dora where you can do her any harm."

Josiah Crabtree's face became a trifle pale.

"Boy, what do you wish to do—ruin me?"

"Mr. Crabtree, you are ruining yourself."

"You were the means of putting me in jail before—you and your brothers."

"You deserved it, didn't you?"

"No."

"I think you did. But that has nothing to do with the present situation. I want to know if you are willing to come to terms or not?"

"What—er—terms do you want me to make?"

"Are you in control of this boat?'

"I am."

"Then, in the first place, you must turn the control of the boat over to me."

"And after that?"

"You can remain on board, if you behave yourself, until we reach the mainland."

"And what then?"

"After that you can make your own terms with Mrs. Stanhope and Dora."

"But the authorities—"

"Mr. Crabtree, for the sake of the Stanhopes we wish to avoid all publicity," replied Tom, playing his game as skillfully as possible. "I don't think they will want to bring you and themselves into court, if you will promise to leave them alone in the future."

"Who is with you here?" And Crabtree looked ashore anxiously.

"Sam is close at hand."

"And the others?"

"Never mind about the others. I hold a winning hand, but what that is I'll let time show. Now, for the last time, are you willing to let me take charge or not?"

"It is a very unusual proceeding."

"Say yes or no."

"What shall I say? I do not wish any trouble."

"Then I am going to take charge. Call up the two sailors who have been running this boat for you."

With a dark look on his face Josiah Crabtree did as requested. At the same time Tom beckoned to Sam to come on the deck.

The sailors were much astonished to see the two strangers. Only the fat tar could speak English, and he translated what was said into French for his companion's benefit.

It was with very bad grace that Josiah Crabtree told the sailor who commanded the *Wellington* that Tom would now direct the movements of the vessel.

"We have—er—decided to change our plans," said the former school- teacher.

"What you lak to do den, hey?" demanded the fat sailor.

"What is the nearest American town to here?" asked Tom.

"Ze nearest place?"

"Yes."

"Buryport."

"And how far is that from here?"

"Ten or eleven miles."

"Then we will sail for that place, and at once."

At this Crabtree looked surprised.

"You are going to Buryport at once? What about the others you said were with you?"

"I will answer no questions." Tom turned around and winked at Sam, who had heard the previous conversation. "I guess they'll follow right enough, eh?"

"Sure," answered Sam. "Dick knows what he's doing, and so does that detective."

"A detective!" groaned Josiah Crabtree. "Has it come to this!" And he wrung his hands nervously.

"Mr. Crabtree, I must ask you to step forward," went on Tom. "I do not wish you to go below."

"Why?"

"I do not wish you to worry Mrs. Stanhope," answered the youth. But what he was afraid of was that Crabtree might take it into his head to arm himself and bring on further trouble.

"As you please," answered the former teacher, with a shrug of his shoulders. "You seem to have matters well in hand." And he strode forward, biting his lip in vexation. He would have tried to escape to the island, only he was afraid no one would ever come to rescue him.

While speaking, Tom had taken the pains to display the pistol taken from the sailor at the cave. Sam now took up a short iron bar lying near, and both boys showed that they meant to remain masters of the situation. The Canadians noted this, but said nothing, for they felt something was wrong and they wished to get into no trouble. A few minutes later the anchor was brought up, the sails hoisted, and the *Wellington* stood away from Needle Point Island.

CHAPTER XXII

THE SECRET OF THE ISLAND CAVE

It is now time that we go back to the *Rocket* and see how Dick and those with him were faring.

At the announcement that a schooner looking like the *Peacock* was in sight he ran on deck with all speed, and caught up a glass belonging to the owner of the steam tug.

"It's the *Peacock*, sure," he cried.

"See anything o' that Captain Langless or them Baxters?" asked Luke Peterson.

"I see somebody, but we are too far off to make out their faces."

The order was passed to the engineer of the tug, and the speed of the craft was materially increased.

But before they could come up to the schooner she disappeared around a headland of the island.

"We must run out a bit," said Captain Parsons. "There is a nasty reef here, and if we aint careful we'll get aground."

Arthur M. Winfield

"Where do you suppose the *Peacock* has gone?" asked Dick.

"Into one of the bays, most likely."

"Can we follow her?"

"Of coarse. The tug doesn't draw any more water than the schooner, if as much."

"Perhaps we had better see how the land lays before we approach too close," suggested Peterson. "They may be prepared to fight us off."

"That is true," said Dick. "Perhaps we can slip into another bay close by."

So it was arranged, and they sped on their way, passing the bay in which the *Peacock* lay.

Near the island was a quantity of driftwood, and they had just gotten out of sight of the bay when there was a sudden grinding and crashing sound on board of the tug, and the engineer shut off the steam power.

"A breakdown!" exclaimed the captain, and so it proved. The screw had become entangled in the limb of a tree, and sufficient damage had been done to render the screw useless.

This was indeed an unlooked-for accident, and Dick wondered what they had best do.

"We can't use the screw at all?" he asked of the engineer, after an examination.

"Not until I have had a chance to repair it."

"And how long will the repairs take?"

"Can't tell till I get at work. Maybe an hour or two, maybe half a day."

This was dismaying information, and Dick held a consultation with Larry Colby and Luke.

"I know what I'd do," said Larry. "I'd have the captain of the tug land me at some point above here, and then I'd watch the *Peacock* from behind some bushes on shore."

This was considered good advice, and Dick agreed to act upon it. He spoke to Parsons, and a small boat was put out, and Dick, Larry, and Peterson were rowed to land.

"Now what will you do with the tug?" asked the eldest Rover.

"We'll haul her in to a safe spot," answered Parsons. "I don't believe those repairs will take over a couple of hours. Then we'll be at your service again."

Once on land Dick led the way into the woods, moving in the direction of the bay where he had last seen the *Peacock*.

He was armed, and so were his companions, but they wished, if possible, to avoid all trouble.

They had landed at a spot where the rocks were numerous and the ground uncertain, and they had not proceeded far when Luke Peterson called a halt.

"We want to be careful here," he said. "This island is full of caves and pitfalls and, before you know it, you'll break a leg."

"It is certainly an ideal hiding place," returned Larry. "Hi, Dick! what's that?"

"What's what?"

"I thought I saw somebody in the brush yonder."

Dick shook his head.

"I saw nothing."

"Neither did I," put in the lumberman. "Who did it look like?"

"Perhaps I was mistaken and it was a bird flitting through the brush. Come on."

Larry plunged ahead and Dick followed.

Both had hardly taken a dozen steps when each gave a yell.

"What's up now?" cried Peterson, and came after them at a bound.

Then all tried to scramble back.

It was too late. They had struck a tiny water-course between the rocks. And now the very bottom of it seemed to drop out, and they sank down and down into almost utter darkness.

"We are lost!" spluttered Dick, but it is doubtful if either of his companions heard him.

For the minute after Dick was so dazed and bewildered that he said nothing more. He clutched at rocks, dirt, and tree roots, but all gave way at his touch.

At last he found himself flat on his back on a heap of dead leaves and moss. Partly across him lay Larry, while Peterson was several feet away. Around the three lay dirt and bushes and several good-sized stones. It was lucky the stones had not come down on top of them, otherwise one or another might have been killed.

"Gosh, what a tumble!" ejaculated Peterson, when he could speak. "I told ye to be careful. This island is like a reg'lar honeycomb fer holes."

"Oh, my foot!" gasped Larry, as he tried to get up.

"That was a tumble and no mistake," said Dick. "What's the matter with your foot, Larry?"

"I don't know, excepting I must have sprained my ankle," was the answer. "Oh!" And Larry gave a loud groan.

Forgetful of their situation, Dick and the lumberman bent over Larry and helped him to get off his shoe and sock. His ankle was beginning to swell and turn red, and he had sprained it beyond a doubt.

The water was coming into the opening from the little stream overhead, and Dick readily procured a hatful of the fluid and the ankle was bathed with this. After this it was bound up, and Larry said it felt somewhat better.

"But I can't walk very far on it," he continued, and then added, with a sorry smile, "I am laid up, just as the *Rocket* is!"

"The question is, now we are down at the bottom of this hole, how are we going to get out?" said Dick to Peterson.

"We'll have to get out some way," was the unsatisfactory response. "See, the water is coming in faster than ever."

The lumberman was right, the water had been running in a tiny stream not larger than a child's wrist; now it was pouring in steadily like a cataract. Soon the bottom of the hole had formed a pool several inches deep.

"Wait till it fills up and then swim out," suggested Larry.

"No, thanks," returned Dick. "We might be drowned by that operation."

The hole was irregular in shape, about ten feet in diameter and fully twenty feet deep. What had caused the sudden sinking was a mystery until it was solved by the water in the pool suddenly dropping away into another hole still deeper. Then of a sudden the trio went down again, this time at an angle, to find themselves in a good-sized cave, where all was dark and uncertain.

The tumble had wrenched Larry's ankle still more, and the youth could not suppress his groans of pain.

As soon as he was able Peterson leaped up, struck a match, and lit some brushwood which happened to be near and which the water had not yet touched.

By this light Larry's ankle was again attended to and bound up in a couple of handkerchiefs.

"If we keep on we'll get to the center of the earth," remarked Dick, as he gazed around curiously. "Where do you suppose we are now?"

"In one of the island caves," answered Peterson. "I told you the place was full of them. That's the reason the smugglers used to hold out here."

"Perhaps we'll come across some of their treasures."

At this Peterson shook his head. "Not likely. When the last of the smugglers was arrested the government detectives searched the island thoroughly and gathered in all to be found."

"I see. Well, how are we to get out, now we are down here?"

"We might climb back, Rover, the way we came, but that is dangerous on account of the water. I rather think we'll do better to look for the regular opening to the cave, if there is any."

The matter was talked over for several minutes, and it was decided that Dick and Peterson should investigate, while Larry remained by the fire, keeping it as bright as possible and resting his sore ankle.

At a short distance ahead the cave branched into two parts, and coming to the forks, Dick took the right while Peterson moved to the left. Dick carried a torch, which he held overhead, and likewise a pistol, in case any snake or wild animal should attack him.

The youth had not proceeded far before he came upon signs which showed that the cave at one time had been inhabited by human beings. First he espied a part of an old bag, then a weather-beaten sailor's cap, and soon after a rusty pistol, falling apart for the want of care.

"This must have been a smugglers' retreat sure," he murmured to himself. "My, if I should stumble across a box of gold!"

He hurried forward and presently reached a spot where the cave broadened out into a round chamber. Here there were a rude table and several benches, all ready to fall apart from decay.

Arthur M. Winfield

With quick steps he approached the table, for he had seen something lying upon it—something which made him start and give a cry of wonder.

In the center of the table was a heap of silver dollars, and beside this was a land map, drawn by hand. On the map lay a rusty dagger and a human skull!

CHAPTER XXIII

THE BAXTERS ARE FOLLOWED

"Well, I never!"

Dick gazed at the silver, the map, the daggers and the skull with mingled surprise and horror.

How had those things come there, and what was the mystery concerning them?

Coming closer, he picked up several of the dollars and examined them. All were dated thirty to forty years back.

Then he picked up the dagger, a beautiful affair of polished steel with a curiously wrought handle of buckhorn.

The skull he left untouched.

The map was covered with dust, some of which he endeavored to blow away. Beneath he saw that there were odd tracings of many kinds, and lettering's in a language which was strange to him. Then his light began to go out and he shouted for Peterson to join him.

The sound echoed and re-echoed throughout the cavern, showing that the place was even more roomy than he had anticipated. He waited several minutes, then saw Peterson's light.

"What's up?" demanded the lumberman as he approached. "Find anything important?"

"I should say so," answered Dick. "Look there."

Peterson did so, then gave a cry of astonishment.

"Silver, lad, silver! And a skull!"

"There is some story hidden in this affair," said Dick soberly. "Can you explain it?"

"I cannot." Peterson picked up the dagger. "That's a French weapon."

"But the dollars are U. S. money."

"Right. It is a mystery and no error. How much money is there here?"

The two counted the pile and found it footed up to two hundred and forty dollars.

"Not a fortune, but still a tidy sum," said Peterson. To a man in his standing two hundred and forty dollars was quite an amount.

"A fair share of it is yours," said Dick. "Let us investigate some more."

The lumberman was willing, and lighting a fresh torch, they moved around the circular chamber. At one point they saw an opening leading into a second chamber. Here were a number of boxes and casks, all covered with dust and dirt, the accumulation of years. Prying open one of the boxes which was handy, they discovered that it contained canned vegetables. A second box contained dress goods, and a third some candles. A cask close at hand was marked "Cognac."

"This was a regular smugglers' hangout," said Peterson. "Those boxes must contain stuff of some value. Rover, we have made a haul by coming here."

"Yes, but I am forgetting all about my brothers," added Dick hastily. "Let us leave this alone for the present. I guess it is safe enough."

"No doubt, since it has rested undisturbed so many years."

They left the storeroom, as it may properly be termed, and returned to the circular chamber.

At first they could find no further opening, but then Dick saw a thin shaft of light coming from a corner. Here there was a flat rock which was easily pulled aside. A broad opening led upward to the outer world.

"Safe, so far as getting out is concerned," remarked Peterson. "All told, I reckon we had quite a lucky tumble, after all."

"If Larry's ankle isn't too bad."

They hurried back to where Larry had been left, and found him still nursing his ankle, which had swollen to the size of his knee. He tried to stand upon it, but the pain was so great he was glad enough to sit down again.

He listened in open-mouthed wonder to what Dick had to tell. "A treasure cave!" he cried. "Who would have dreamed of such a thing on Lake Huron!"

Arthur M. Winfield

Now that Larry could not move, the others were in a quandary as to what to do. Dick was impatient to be after the *Peacock*.

"The folks on the schooner may take it into their heads to sail away, if they caught sight of the steam tug," he said. "And if they give us the slip I won't know where to look for them."

"I guess I'll be safe if left alone," said Larry. "I have water and the fire, and my pistol. You go ahead, and come back for me when it is convenient. Only don't leave the island without me."

"Leave without you? Not much!" answered Dick.

"You forget the treasure," put in Peterson, with a laugh. "We are not going to let that slip."

"That's so," said Larry. "All right; I'll remain as the guardian of the treasure." And so it was arranged.

It was no easy matter to gain the outer air once more, for the passageway was choked with dirt and brushwood which the wind had blown in. When they came into the open they found themselves close to the lake shore at a spot surrounded thickly with trees.

"A fine cove for a smuggler to hide in," observed Peterson. "No wonder they made this cave their rendezvous."

"Where is the bay in which the *Peacock* disappeared?"

"To the westward, Rover. Come, I'll show the way."

"Be careful that we don't get into another trap."

"I've got my eyes open," responded the lumberman.

On they went once more, over the rocks and through a tangle of brushwood. It was now almost dark, and Dick was beginning to think they would lose their way when Peterson called a sudden halt.

"Here we are," he whispered and pointed ahead. There, through the trees, could be seen the waters of the tiny bay, and there lay the *Peacock* at anchor.

Only one man was on deck, a sailor Dick had seen several times. Otherwise the craft appeared deserted.

"Do you suppose the Baxters and the others have gone ashore?" asked Dick.

"No telling yet, lad. Let us watch out for a while."

They sat down and watched until the darkness of night began to hide the *Peacock* from view.

At last they saw Arnold Baxter come on deck, followed by Dan.

The two entered a rowboat and a sailor took them ashore. They had scarcely landed when Captain Langless appeared, coming along a pathway but a few yards from where Dick and the lumberman were in hiding.

At once a wordy war ensued between the Baxters and the owner of the schooner. What it was about Dick and Peterson could not make out, although they realized that it concerned Tom and Sam.

"Your men are a set of doughheads," cried Arnold Baxter. "They are to be trusted with nothing."

"Never mind, we'll come out ahead anyway," retorted Captain Langless. "I reckon you've been tripped up yourself before this."

"I warned you to be careful."

"It wasn't my fault."

"What's to do now?" put in Dan Baxter. "Shall we stay on the island, dad?"

"Certainly," grumbled Arnold Baxter. "But I don't know exactly what to do," and the man scratched his head in perplexity.

"Let us go up to the cave."

"That won't do you any good," growled Captain Langless. "I know what I am going to do."

"What?"

"I'm going to sail around the island and find out if any other boat is near. I don't want those boys to signal another boat."

"A good idea," said Arnold Baxter. "But Dan and I can remain on shore anyway."

"Just as you please," and Captain Langless shrugged his shoulders.

The rowboat was still at the shore, and the captain returned to the *Peacock* with the member of his crew, leaving the Baxters to themselves.

Dick nudged Peterson in the side.

"Can it be possible that Tom and Sam have escaped?" he whispered.

"It looks that way," answered the lumberman. "Anyway, something is very much wrong or these rascals wouldn't fall out with each other."

"Hadn't we better watch the Baxters?"

"I think so. The *Peacock* will not go far, I'm pretty sure of that."

The Baxters now passed along the footpath leading to the cave in which Tom and Sam had been placed.

Noiselessly Dick and Peterson followed. As Dick advanced he drew his pistol.

Quarter of a mile was covered and they were close to the cave, when Arnold Baxter suddenly halted.

"Dan, supposing Captain Langless doesn't come back," he exclaimed, loud enough for Dick and his companion to hear.

"Doesn't come back!" ejaculated the bully. "Why, he's got to come back."

"No, he hasn't."

"But I don't understand—"

"You know well enough that the Rovers tried to bribe the captain."

"Yes, but they ran away—"

"Perhaps it's only a bluff, Dan. The boys may have been taken to another part of the island, from which Langless can transfer them to the schooner later."

"What, and desert us!" groaned the bully.

"Yes, and desert us. I think we were foolish to leave the *Peacock* without taking the captain or Cadmus along. I won't trust any of them any longer."

"Well, what shall we do, dad; go back?"

"It's too late now. The *Peacock* has gotten under way long ago."

"Well, let us try to get on the track of the two boys. Perhaps we can follow them up from the cave. If all of the footsteps point this way we'll know the captain has been deceiving us."

Again the Baxters moved on, and so did Dick and Peterson. The way was rough and made Dan grumble a good deal.

"We ought to have kept this game all in our own hands from the start," said the former bully of Putnam Hall. "We made a rank mistake to take Captain Langless into our confidence."

"I won't care if only we make Anderson Rover pony up that money," answered the father. "I'm afraid the mine scheme will have to fall through."

"What did you strike him for in cash?"

"Ten thousand dollars."

"You ought to have made it fifty."

"I wanted to get ten first and double that afterward. If I struck him too high first I was afraid he wouldn't try to meet me, but put the detectives on the track without delay."

Arthur M. Winfield

CHAPTER XXIV

AN ENCOUNTER IN THE DARK

A little while later the Baxters reached the cave where Tom and Sam had been held prisoners.

The sailor who had been left bound had long since been released, so the place was deserted.

"Look out for snakes," said Dan. "We had better light torches."

This was done, for it was now dark under the trees.

Hiding in a thicket, Dick and Peterson saw the Baxters enter the cave. The pair remained inside for fully quarter of an hour, and came out looking much disappointed.

With torches close to the ground they searched for Sam and Tom's trail.

"Here are footprints!" exclaimed Arnold Baxter, at last. "They are not made by men, either."

"They must be the boys'," answered Dan. "Come on, let us follow."

"It is very dark, Dan. I'm afraid we'll have to wait until morning."

Nevertheless, the pair passed on, and again Dick and Peterson came behind.

Hardly three rods had been passed when Dan Baxter let out a cry as some small wild animal dashed across the trail. The bully turned to run, and discovered Dick ere the latter could hide.

"Dick Rover!" he gasped.

"Rover!" cried Arnold Baxter. "What are you talking about, Dan?"

"Here is Dick Rover! And that lumber fellow is with him."

"Impossible! Why, Rover, where did you come from?" And Arnold Baxter came up, hardly believing his eyes.

"We were following you, Arnold Baxter," answered Dick quietly.

"For what?"

"To see what you were going to do next?"

"Have you found Sam and Tom?" questioned Dan quickly.

"Dan, be still!" thundered his father. "You are always putting your foot into it."

"I reckon you chaps are fairly caught," put in Luke Peterson.

"Caught?" came from both, in a breath.

"Yes, caught," said Dick. "We did not follow you for nothing."

"Perhaps you are the ones who are caught," said Arnold Baxter, with a sickly smile.

"Hardly," and Dick showed his pistol. "We are well armed, Arnold Baxter, and will stand no fooling."

"We are armed, too—" began Dan, but his parent stopped him.

"Of course you came to this island on a boat of some sort," went on the elder Baxter.

"How else could we come? The mainland is miles away."

"Where is your boat?"

"Not far off, and well manned, too," added Dick. "We came not alone to capture you, but also the *Peacock* and all on board."

At this announcement the faces of the Baxters fell, and Dan actually trembled.

"Where is your boat?" repeated Arnold Baxter.

"As I just told you, not far off. The question is, will you submit quietly, or must I summon help?"

"Submit to what?"

"Submit to being taken to our boat."

"You have no right to make me go to your boat."

"I'll be hanged if I'll go," growled Dan.

"And you may be shot if you don't go," answered Dick significantly. "I know you well, and I shall take no further chances with you. Now will you go or not?"

"I suppose, if we don't go, you'll bring some officers here to compel us to do as you wish."

"Exactly."

"You may as well give in," said Peterson. "This island is not large, and even if you try to run away you'll be found, sooner or later. The *Peacock* is probably already captured, and those on our boat will see that no other boat comes near here until we have you safe on board. The jig is up."

"I won't give in!" cried Arnold Baxter. "Come, Dan!" He caught his son by the arm, and both turned and sped into the nearest brush.

It was dark, the torches having died low, and before Dick could shoot, even if he wished to do so, the pair of rascals were out of sight.

"Stop!" said Dick to Peterson, who was for following them up. "We can do nothing in the darkness. Let them go. To-morrow is another day. Let us return to the *Rocket* and take steps to capture the *Peacock*."

"Yes, and we must get back to Larry," said the lumberman.

It was no easy matter to find their way back to the treasure cave, and they missed the direction half a dozen times. When they did get back it was so gloomy in the bushes that they had to call out to Larry, in order to locate him.

"Gracious! I was afraid you would never come back," said the youth.

"We've had quite an adventure," replied Dick, and related the particulars.

Larry's ankle was somewhat better, and by leaning on both Dick and Peterson he managed to hobble along to where the *Rocket's* small boat had landed them.

The steam tug was close at hand, and they were soon on board.

"Is the screw repaired?" was Dick's first question.

"Not quite, but it will be inside of half an hour," answered Jack Parsons.

"Have you seen anything of the *Peacock*? She is sailing around the island."

"No, haven't seen any sail since you left. We—"

A cry from the lookout interrupted the captain.

"Here comes the *Peacock*!"

The report was true, and all crowded forward to catch sight of the schooner in the darkness.

The stars made it fairly light on the water and, as the schooner came up close to the steam tug, Dick made out several figures on board.

"Ahoy, what tug is that?" came from the schooner.

"The *Rocket*" answered Parsons. "What schooner is that?"

To this there was no answer.

"What are you doing here?" asked Captain Langless instead.

"We are in trouble," returned Parsons, after whispering with Dick.

"What's up?"

"We've had a breakdown."

"Seen anybody from the island?"

"Why, we thought this island was deserted."

"So it is."

"Come up closer and give us a lift."

"Can't, we are behind time now."

Then, without warning, a Bengal light was lit on board of the schooner. A large reflector was placed behind the light, which was thus cast on the deck of the *Rocket*. At once Dick, Peterson, and the others were exposed to the gaze of Captain Langless.

"Ha! I suspected as much!" roared the master of the schooner. "Sheer off, Wimble, or the game is up!"

The helm of the *Peacock* was at once thrown over, and she began to move off. A stiff breeze caused her to make rapid progress.

"Stop!" cried Dick. "Stop, or we will fire on you!"

He had scarcely spoken when the report of a pistol rang out

and a bullet cut through the air over his head.

"Let that be a warning to you to leave us alone!" cried Captain Langless.

Then the schooner increased her speed, the flare from the Bengal light died out, and soon the *Peacock* was lost to view in the darkness.

CHAPTER XXV

BEACHING THE "WELLINGTON"

"How is this for a turn of fortune?" remarked Tom, as he and Sam stood on the deck of the *Wellington* and watched the shore of Needle Point Island fading from view in the distance.

"It's all right, if only we can make those Canadians obey us," replied the youngest of the Rovers. "They don't seem to like matters much. They look dark and distrustful."

"I don't think they'll make trouble, Sam."

"Josiah Crabtree seems thoroughly cowed."

"Don't trust him. He is worse than a snake in the grass and he hates us worse than poison."

The two paced the deck thoughtfully. Mrs. Stanhope was still in the cabin, in the company of one of the sailors' wives, while the former teacher of Putnam Hall also kept out of sight.

"This seems an old tub of a boat," went on Tom, a few minutes later. "I wonder that Crabtree didn't hire something better. She just crawls along, and no more."

Arthur M. Winfield

"Probably he got the boat cheap. He always was the one to go in for cheap things." And in his surmise the lad was correct.

It was not long before one of the Canadians took hold of a hand-pump near the bow of the boat and began to pump the water out of the hold.

"Hullo, your old tub leaks, eh?" said Tom.

"Yees, heem leak some," answered the fat Canadian. "Heem want some what-you-call-heem, tar; hey?" And he smiled broadly.

"Any danger of sinking?"

At this the Canadian shook his head. Then he went to pumping at a faster rate than ever.

"I believe he is afraid," said Tom to Sam. "She must leak fearfully, or he wouldn't pump up so much water."

"Well, the journey to the mainland won't last forever— that's one satisfaction, Tom. I reckon the tub is good for that much of a run. I don't care what becomes of her after we are ashore."

"Nor I. She can sink if she wishes, with Crabtree on board, too."

"Sink!" cried a voice behind them. "Is there danger of the ship going down? I noticed that she was leaking yesterday."

It was Josiah Crabtree who spoke. He had just come up and he was very pale.

"I guess she'll keep up a few minutes longer," said Tom soberly.

"A few minutes! Oh, dear! if we did sink what would become of us?"

"Why, if we did sink we'd sink, that's all."

"I mean, if the ship sunk what would we do?"

"You might wade ashore, if your legs are long enough."

"But this is no joking matter, Thomas. The lake is very deep out here."

"Then you had better find a life-preserver."

Josiah Crabtree gave something of a groan and moved away. He did not know whether Tom was poking fun at him or not. Yet he did search for a preserver—and in doing that he was wiser than the boys had anticipated.

Presently the wind veered around and the yards came over with a bang. The *Wellington* gave a lurch, and there was a strange creaking and cracking far below the deck. The Canadian pumped more madly than ever, and shouted to his companion in French.

"Is she leaking worse?" asked Tom.

The Canadian nodded. Then the *Wellington* gave another lurch, and Tom noticed that her bow gave an odd little dip.

"Filling with water, I'll be bound," he muttered, and running to the hatch he sounded the well hole. There were sixteen inches of water below. Soon it measured seventeen inches.

"We've sprung a bad leak," he announced to Sam. "It looks as if we might go to the bottom."

"Oh, Tom, you don't mean it!"

"Yes, I do."

"Can't we turn back? The island isn't more than two miles off. It may be safer to go back than to keep on."

"Exactly my idea, Sam. I'll speak to the Canadian about it."

The fat sailor was still pumping, but his face was full of despair.

"De ship he go down," he gasped. "We drown in ze lake!"

"Better turn back to the island," returned Tom. "And lose no time about it."

"Yees! yees! zat ees best. We turn heem back!"

The Canadian shouted to his companion, who was at the wheel, and then left the pump to attend to the sails. At once Tom took his place at the pump, at the same time calling to Sam to go down for Mrs. Stanhope.

"Tell her to come on deck," he said. "And find some life-preservers, if you can."

"What of the rowboat?"

"It's as rotten as the ship, Sam. We'll have to swim for it, if this tub sinks."

Sam disappeared into the cabin and Tom turned to the pumping. Never had he worked so hard, and the perspiration poured down his face. Soon Mrs. Stanhope appeared, her face full of fear.

"Oh, pray Heaven we do not go down!" she murmured. "How far are we from land?"

"We have turned back for the island," answered Tom, hardly able to speak because of his exertions. "We are not much more than a mile away."

"A mile! And how long will it take us to reach the island?"

"About ten minutes, if the wind holds out."

The *Wellington* was now groaning and creaking in every timber, as if she was aware that her last hour on the surface of the lake had come. She was, as Tom had said, an old "tub," and should have been condemned years before. But the Canadians were used to her and handled the craft as skillfully as possible. They, too, provided themselves with life-preservers and, when Sam relieved his brother at the pump, Tom did likewise.

As she filled with water the ship moved more slowly until, despite the breeze, she seemed to merely crawl along. It was now growing dark and the island was not yet in sight.

Sounded again, the well hole showed twenty inches of water. At this the fat Canadian gave a long sigh and disappeared into the forecastle, to obtain a trunk and some of his other belongings. Sam had already brought on deck the things belonging to Mrs. Stanhope.

At last the fat sailor uttered a welcome cry. "The island! The island!"

"Where?" questioned the others.

The sailor pointed with his hand. He was right; land was just visible, and no more. Then of a sudden came a crash and a shock which threw all of those on board headlong.

"We have struck a rock!" yelled Josiah Crabtree. "We are going down!" And in his terror he leaped overboard and struck out wildly for the distant shore.

Sam was also ready, in a moment, to spring into the water, but Tom held him back. The *Wellington* settled and swung around, and then sheered off the rock and went on her way. But it was plainly to be seen that she could float but a few minutes more at the most.

"There is a sandy shore!" cried Tom to the Canadians. "Better drive her straight in and beach her!"

"Good!" said the fat sailor, and spoke to his companion in French. Then, as well as they were able, they brought the water-logged craft around to the wind. Slowly she drifted in, her deck sinking with every forward move. Then came a strong pull of wind which caught the sails squarely and drove them ahead. A grating and a slishing followed, and they ran up the muddy shore and came to a standstill in about three feet of water.

"Hurrah! saved!" shouted Sam. "My, but that was a narrow escape!"

"Where is Mr. Crabtree?" asked Mrs. Stanhope anxiously. "Oh, do not let him drown!"

They looked around and saw him in the water not a hundred feet away, puffing and blowing like a porpoise.

"Save me!" he screamed, as soon as he saw their safety. "Don't let me drown!"

"You're all right," returned Tom. "It's shallow here. See if you can't walk ashore."

Josiah Crabtree continued his paddling, and presently put down his feet very gingerly. He could just touch the bottom. Soon he was in a position to walk, and lost no time in getting out of the lake and coming up to the bow of the *Wellington.*

"Oh, dear, this is dreadful!" he groaned, with a shiver. "Throw out a plank that I may come onboard."

"Thought you were tired of the old tub," said Tom dryly.

"I thought she was surely going down, Thomas. Please throw out a plank, that's a good boy."

The Canadian got the longest plank at hand and, resting one end at the bow, allowed the other to fall ashore, in a few inches of mud and water. Then Josiah Crabtree came up the plank on hands and knees, looking for all the world like a half-drowned rat.

CHAPTER XXVI

CRABTREE JOINS THE BAXTERS

"Well, we are no better off than we were before," remarked Sam, after Josiah Crabtree had disappeared in the direction of the cabin and the two boys had walked forward by themselves.

"No, we are no better off, but we have succeeded in rescuing Mrs. Stanhope from old Crabtree's clutches, and that is something."

"True, but supposing we fall in the hands of the Baxters and Captain Langless again?"

"Can't we hold them at bay, if they try to come on board this tub?"

"Perhaps. But we can't remain on board the *Wellington* forever."

Now that the danger was over the lads found that they were hungry, and called upon the sailors to bring out what food the craft afforded. They made a hearty meal, in which Mrs. Stanhope joined. Josiah Crabtree was not invited, and had to eat later on with the sailors and the one sailor's wife.

"This wreck may throw us together for some time, Crabtree," said Tom, later on, when he and the former school-teacher were alone. "I want to warn you to behave yourself during that time."

"I know my own business," was the stiff reply.

"Well, you keep your distance, or there will be trouble."

"Can I not speak to Mrs. Stanhope?"

"When she speaks to you, yes. But you must not bother her with your attentions. And if you try your hypnotic nonsense we'll pitch you overboard," and so speaking, Tom walked off again. Josiah Crabtree looked very black, nevertheless he took the youth's words to heart and only spoke to Mrs. Stanhope when it was necessary.

By the time supper was over it was night and time to think of getting some rest. The boys took possession of one of the staterooms on board, and arranged that each should sleep five hours, Tom taking the first watch. Mrs. Stanhope soon retired, and so did Josiah Crabtree and one of the Canadians.

Tom found the fat Canadian, the man to remain on deck, quite a sociable fellow, and asked him much about himself and how he had come to hire out with Crabtree. He soon discovered that the Canadians were honest to the last degree, and had gone in for the trip thinking all was above-board.

"I soon see ze man haf von bad eye," said the Canadian. "I tell Menot I no like heem. Now he has brought ruin on our ship."

The Canadian imagined that Crabtree had hypnotized the

Arthur M. Winfield

sailing qualities of the *Wellington* as well as cast a spell over Mrs. Stanhope, and Tom saw no reason, just then, for saying anything to the contrary.

"You must watch Crabtree," he said. "Don't let him get you in his power. Stick by me and my brother, and you will be all right," and the Canadian promised.

"But who vill pay for ze ship?" he questioned dolefully. "'Tis all Menot and myself haf in ze worl'!" And he shook his head in sorrow.

"We will pay you well for whatever you do for us. The balance you must get out of Crabtree." Then Tom gave the fat sailor a five-dollar bill, and from that moment the pair were warm friends.

Feeling that Crabtree would not dare to do much as matters stood, Tom did not take the trouble to arouse Sam when he turned in, and the brothers slept soundly until some time after sunrise.

"Say, why didn't you wake me up?" asked Sam in astonishment. "You didn't stay up all night, did you?"

"Not much!" answered Tom, and spoke of the Canadian, whose name was Peglace.

"Well, what's to do?"

"I must confess I don't know. I suppose the Baxters and Captain Langless are on the search for us."

"More than likely."

"Then we had better lay low until some vessel comes to rescue us."

"I don't think very many ships come this way."

"Neither do I, but we won't despair. Come, I'm hungry again," and they stirred around to get breakfast.

An examination showed that the *Wellington* was hard and fast in the mud, and likely to remain exactly as she stood for an indefinite time. Wading around in the water below, the Canadians reported several planks broken and wrenched loose, and that immediate repairs seemed out of the question,

"Ze ship ees gone," said Peglace sadly. "We air like zat man, what-you-call-heem, Crusoe Robinson, hey?" And he shook his head.

"Well, I hope we don't have to stay as long on this island as Robinson Crusoe remained on that other," remarked Sam. "Tom, I'm going for a walk on shore."

"Can I go with you?" put in Josiah Crabtree humbly. "I am tired of this ship's deck."

"All right, come on."

"I will remain with Mrs. Stanhope," said Tom. "Don't go too far, Sam."

Sam and the former teacher of Putnam Hall were soon over the side. The boy came down the plank easily enough, but Crabtree slipped and went into the water and mud up to his knees.

"Ugh! I am always unfortunate!" he spluttered. "However, since the weather is warm, I don't think I'll suffer much."

At a short distance up the beach there was a headland,

Arthur M. Winfield

covered with tall trees. Sam decided to make his way to this.

"I'm going to climb the tallest of the trees and look around," he said. "You can go along, if you wish."

"I will go, but I cannot climb the tree," answered Crabtree.

To get to the headland they had to make a detour around a marshy spot and then climb over a number of rough rocks. The exertion exhausted Josiah Crabtree, and he soon fell behind.

Reaching the headland, Sam gazed around anxiously. He could see a long distance to the north and the west, but not a sail was in sight.

"The *Peacock* ought to be somewhere around here," he told himself, and then, coming to a tall tree with low, drooping branches, he began to climb to the top.

It was a difficult task, for the tree was a thickly wooded one and a veritable monarch of the forest. But he persevered, and at last gained the topmost branch.

Here the view of the island and its vicinity was much extended, and he could see not only the bay where the *Peacock* had been at anchor, but also several other harbors.

"The *Peacock* is gone!" Such were the first words which escaped him. "She must have left the island altogether!"

With anxious eye he turned his gaze to the other harbors, and suddenly gave a start.

"A steam tug! How lucky!" He had discovered the *Rocket*, which was just getting up steam in order to follow the *Peacock*; the screw being now repaired and ready for use.

As fast as he could he descended to the ground, his one thought being to tell Tom of his discovery, and to either get to the steam tug or to signal those on board, so that the tug might not leave the island without them. He had noticed the black smoke curling up from the stack, and knew that this betokened that steam was getting up.

"Sam Rover!"

The voice came from behind the rocks, like a bolt out of the clear sky. Then Dan Baxter rushed forward, followed by his father.

Sam was taken off his guard, and before he could do anything the Baxters had him by both arms and were holding him a prisoner.

"Let me go!"

"Not much!" came from Arnold Baxter. "Where are your brothers—I mean," he added, in some confusion, "where is Tom?"

"Find out for yourself, Arnold Baxter. Let me go, I say!" And Sam began to struggle.

"Daniel Baxter, is it possible!" came in Josiah Crabtree's voice, and he emerged from the brushwood. "What an extraordinary meeting!"

"I should say it was!" responded the bully. "Where did you spring from?"

"Perhaps, Daniel, I can ask the same question."

"Is Tom Rover with you?"

"No, he is on a ship which is beached a short distance from here."

"Alone?"

"No, with some Canadians and—er—Mrs. Stanhope."

"Oh, I see! the same old game," growled the bully. "Anybody else on the boat?"

"No."

"If that's the case we are in luck," came from Arnold Baxter. He gazed at Crabtree sharply. "Do you know where this lad came from?"

"What do you mean?"

"He and his brother Tom escaped from us. We brought them here,"

"What! I thought they had followed me and Mrs. Stanhope."

"Hardly." Arnold Baxter proceeded to bind Sam's arms behind him. "Dan, take him to yonder tree and tie him fast." Then he walked away to talk to Josiah Crabtree.

The conversation which followed lasted for quarter of an hour. What was said Sam could not make out. The boy wanted to get away, but was helpless, and now Dan Baxter took away the pistol with which he had provided himself. A little later the Baxters and Crabtree moved toward the wreck, leaving him bound to the tree, alone.

CHAPTER XXVII

HOW TOM WAS CAPTURED

Tom was pacing the deck of the wreck in thoughtful mood when, on looking up, he saw Josiah Crabtree coming back alone.

"Where is Sam?" he called out.

"Samuel wishes you to join him at the headland," replied Crabtree. "He thinks a boat is coming around the other side of the island."

"Did you see it?"

"No, my eyesight is failing me and I had no spectacles along."

"Well, you can go back with me," said Tom, to make sure that the former teacher should not bother Mrs. Stanhope during his absence from the *Wellington*.

"I calculated to go back," responded Crabtree.

Telling Mrs. Stanhope that he would soon return, Tom left the wreck and followed Josiah Crabtree around the marsh land and over the cocks.

Arthur M. Winfield

So long as Crabtree was in front poor Tom did not anticipate any treachery, consequently he was taken completely by surprise when the Baxters fell upon him from behind and bore him to the ground.

"Don't!" he cried, and tried to rise. But Dan Baxter struck him a heavy blow with a club, and then pointed the pistol at his head, and he had to submit.

When he was a prisoner Josiah Crabtree came back, his face beaming sarcastically. "The tables are turned once more, Thomas," he said. "We are masters of the situation. How do you like the prospect?"

"What have you done with Sam?"

"We have taken care of him," answered Arnold Baxter. "And we'll take good care of you after this, too."

Tom said no more, but his heart sank like a lump of lead in his breast. The talk of a ship being in sight must be a hoax, unless Crabtree referred to the *Peacock*.

The Baxters had a small bit of rope remaining, and with this they tied Tom's hands behind him. Then he was made to march to where Sam was a prisoner.

"What, Tom! you too?" cried the youngest Rover. And then he felt worse than ever, for he had hoped that his brother might come to his rescue.

Both boys were tied to the trees, but at some distance apart. Then, without delay, the Baxters and Josiah Crabtree hurried off toward the *Wellington*. The Baxters had heard that the boat was not much damaged, and thought that it might be possible to patch her up sufficiently to reach the mainland, and to do this ere Dick Rover and his party discovered them. For the *Peacock* and Langless Arnold Baxter now cared but little.

"She has left the bay," he said to Dan, "and more than likely has abandoned us."

The Canadians were surprised to see Josiah Crabtree returning with two strangers, and Mrs. Stanhope uttered a shriek when confronted by the Baxters.

"I must be dreaming," she murmured, when she had recovered sufficiently to speak. "How came you here?"

"We are not answering questions just now, madam," said Arnold Baxter. "We wish to patch up this boat if we can, and at once," and he called the Canadians to him.

As can be imagined, the sailors were dumfounded, especially when told that the Rover boys would not be back, at least for the present. They shook their heads.

"Ze ship cannot be patched up," said Peglace. "Ze whole bottom ees ready to fall out."

Arnold Baxter would not believe him, and armed with lanterns he and Dan went below to make an examination.

"What does this mean?" demanded Mrs. Stanhope of Crabtree, when they were left alone. "What have you done with the Rover boys?"

"Do not worry about them, my dear," said the former teacher soothingly. "All will come right in the end."

Then he began to look at her steadily, in an endeavor to bring her once more under his hypnotic influence. But, without waiting, she ran off and refused to confront him again.

"Follow me and I will leap into the lake," she cried, and fearful she would commit suicide, he let her alone.

The examination below decks lasted nearly an hour, and was far from satisfactory to Arnold Baxter. He felt that the *Wellington* might be patched up, but the work would take at least several days, and there was no telling what would happen in the meantime.

"Dick Rover and his party are sure to find us Before that time," said Dan.

"I am afraid so, Dan. But I know of nothing better to do than to remain here."

"We might find the *Peacock* and make a new deal with Captain Langless."

"Langless is a weak-hearted fool, and I'll never trust him again. We would have done much better had we hired a small boat which we could ran alone."

"But what shall we do, dad?"

"I think we had best go into hiding in the interior of the island. We can take a store of provisions along from this boat."

"Shall we take the Rovers with us?"

"We may as well. We can't let them starve, and by holding them prisoners we may be able to make terms with Dick Rover and his friends."

"That's an idea. I reckon Dick will do a lot rather than see Tom and Sam suffer."

"To be sure."

"Where do you suppose Dick Rover and his friends are now?"

"Somewhere around the island, although I have seen nothing of their boat."

By noon the Baxters had completed their plans and left the boat, carrying with them a load of provisions wrapped up in a sheet of canvas. They invited Josiah Crabtree to go with them, but that individual declined.

"I cannot take Mrs. Stanhope along," he said, "and I will not desert the lady."

"As you please," replied Arnold Baxter.

"What are you going to do with Tom and Sam Rover?"

"Take them with us. If you see anything of Dick Rover, don't say anything about us."

"I don't wish to see Dick Rover," answered Josiah Crabtree nervously.

"If the Dick Rover party leaves the island, we'll come back," put in Dan. "In the meantime, if I was you, I'd lay low."

Soon the Baxters were out of sight, and then Josiah Crabtree turned to have another talk with Mrs. Stanhope, in the meantime setting the Canadians on guard, to watch for and hail any passing sail which might appear.

In his wandering on the island Arnold Baxter had stumbled across a convenient cave near the headland where he had encountered Sam Rover, and thither father and son now made their way.

The cave gained they put down their bundles, which included a quantity of rope, and then started for the headland to bring in Tom and Sam.

The headland gained, a surprise awaited than. Both boys had disappeared.

CHAPTER XXVIII

THE BAXTERS TALK IT OVER

"Tom, we are in a fix."

"So it would seem, Sam. Who ever dreamed of running across the Baxters in this fashion?"

"We are in the hands of a trio of rascals now, for Crabtree is as bad as the others."

"Perhaps, but he hasn't the nerve that Arnold Baxter has. What shall we do?"

"Try to get free."

"I can't budge an inch. Dan Baxter took especial delight in tying me up."

"I can move one hand and if—It is free! Hurrah!"

"Can you get the other hand free?"

"I can try. The rope—that's free, too. Now for my legs."

Sam Rover worked rapidly, and was soon as free as ever. Then he ran over to where Tom was tied up and liberated

Arthur M. Winfield

his brother.

"Now, what shall we do?"

"I move we go after the people on that steam tug and get them to help us rescue Mrs. Stanhope."

"That's a good idea, and the quicker we go the better."

Sam remembered very well in what direction he had seen the tug, and now set a straight course across the island to the cove.

But the trail led over a hill and through a dense thicket, and long before the journey was half finished both lads were well-nigh exhausted.

"We ought to have followed the shore around—we would have got there quicker," panted Tom, as he fairly cut his way through the dense brush- wood.

"I hope there are no wild animals here."

"I doubt if there is anything very large on the island. If so, we would have seen it before this."

So speaking, they pushed on once more. The woods passed, they came to a swamp filled with long grass. They hurried around this, and then into the forest skirting the lake shore.

At last the cove came into sight. Alas! the steam tug was nowhere to be seen.

"She has gone!" groaned Sam. "Oh, what luck!

"I can't see a sign of her anywhere?" returned Tom. "She must have steamed away right after you came down the tree."

"More than likely."

Much disappointed and utterly worn out, they cast themselves down in the shade to rest. As they rested they listened intently, but only the breeze through the trees and the soft lap-lap of the waves striking the rocks reached their ears.

"I never thought a spot on our lakes could be so lonely," said Sam at length. "Why, it's as if we were in the middle of the Pacific!"

"I trust no harm befalls Mrs. Stanhope, Sam. Perhaps it is our duty to go back to her, in spite of the danger."

"I was thinking of that, too. But we are only two boys against two men and a boy, and they are armed."

"I think the Canadians will prove our friends in a mix-up. They hate Crabtree, for they half fancy he bewitched their boat."

"We might go back on the sly and do some spying."

"That is what I mean."

But they were too tired to go back at once, and spent a good hour near the beach. Close at hand was a tiny spring, and here they procured a drink of water and took a wash-up, after which they felt somewhat better.

They were about to start on the return when Tom suddenly plucked his brother by the sleeve.

"Somebody is coming," he whispered. "Let us hide."

They had scarcely time to get behind some brushwood

Arthur M. Winfield

when the Baxters came into view, moving very slowly and gazing sharply around them.

"I don't see a thing, dad," came from Dan Baxter in disgusted tones. "I don't believe they came this way."

"They certainly didn't go back to that old boat," replied Arnold Baxter. "Let us take a walk along the beach."

"I am tired to death. Let us rest first."

So speaking, Dan Baxter threw himself on a grassy bank overlooking the lake, and Arnold Baxter followed.

Both were out of sorts and did a large amount of grumbling. The father lit a short briar-root pipe, while the son puffed away at a cigarette,

"I'd give a hundred dollars if a boat would come along and take us to the mainland," observed the father. "I am sick and tired of this game all through."

"So am I sick of it, dad. We made a mistake by ever coming East, it seems to me."

"If I could get to the mainland I might make money out of it even so, Dan. Anderson Rover may have sent that ten thousand dollars to Bay City, after all. He thinks an awful lot of his sons, and won't want a hair of their head harmed."

"So the money was to go to Bay City. You didn't tell me that before."

"I wanted to keep the matter secret."

"Who will receive it there?"

"A man I can trust."

"Oh, pshaw! you needn't be so close-mouthed about it," growled the son, lighting a fresh cigarette.

"Well, the man's name is Cowdrick—Hiram Cowdrick. He comes from Colorado, and used to know the Roebuck crowd."

"I suppose old Rover was to send the money in secret?"

"Certainly. I wrote him a long letter, telling him that if there was the least effort made to follow up the money on his part the lives of his sons should pay the forfeit."

"That's the way to put it, dad. I shouldn't wonder if old Rover sent the money on."

"I'd soon find out, if I could get to shore. If I had the money the boys could rot here, for all I care."

"Thank you for nothing," muttered Tom, under his breath. "Just you wait till I have a chance to square accounts, that's all!"

"Hush!" whispered Sam. "They must not discover us." And then Tom became silent again.

"Josiah Crabtree is in a fix, too," went on Dan, with something of a laugh. "He don't seem to know what to do."

"Where is Mrs. Stanhope's daughter?"

"I don't know. If Crabtree marries Mrs. Stanhope, it will break Dora all up."

"Well, that isn't our affair. But it is queer we should run

together on this island. We can—What is that? A sail!"

Arnold Baxter leaped to his feet, and so did Dan. Tom and Sam also looked in the direction pointed out.

There was a sail, true enough, far out on the lake. All watched it with interest and saw it gradually grow larger. Evidently the craft was heading directly for the island.

"She is coming this way, dad!" almost shouted Dan.

"It looks so to me," replied Arnold Baxter, with increasing interest. "And she isn't the *Peacock*, either."

"No, she's a strange ship—a sloop, by her rig."

The Baxters watched the coming sail eagerly, and it must be confessed that the Rover boys were equally interested.

"If the folks on that boat are honest, they will surely help us against the Baxters," murmured Sam.

"Just what I was thinking," replied his brother.

At last the vessel was near enough to be signaled, and, running to a high rock overlooking the water, Dan swung his hat and a handkerchief in the air.

At first the signals were not seen, but at last came a voice through a speaking trumpet.

"Ahoy, there!"

"Ahoy!" shouted Dan. "Come here! Come here!"

"What's the trouble?"

"We are wrecked. We want you to take us off."

"Wrecked?"

"Yes. Will you take us off?"

"Certainly."

Slowly, but surely, the sloop drew nearer. She was a fair-sized craft, and carried a crew of three. The men seemed to be nice fellows, and not at all of the Captain Langless class. Soon the sloop dropped anchor close in shore and the mainsail came down at the same time.

CHAPTER XXIX

DORA STANHOPE APPEARS

"So you have been shipwrecked?" said the master of the sloop, a young man of apparently twenty-five, whose name was Fairwell.

"Yes," answered Baxter senior.

"Your own boat, or some large vessel?"

"Our own boat. We were out on a little cruise when we struck something in the dark and our craft went down almost immediately. Fortunately we were not far from this shore, or we would have been drowned. Where are you bound?"

"Nowhere in particular. How long have you been on the island?"

"Since night before last?"

"All alone?"

"Yes."

"Had anything to eat?"

"Well—er—not much," stammered Arnold Baxter. "We found some wreckage with some bread and a few cans of sardines, but that is all."

"Then I reckon you won't go back on a square meal?" laughed Fairwell.

"Indeed I won't!" put in Dan, bound to say something.

"We would like to get back to the mainland as soon as possible," went on Arnold Baxter. "I am from Chicago, and must attend to some banking matters. My name is Larson—Henry Larson of State Street."

"Well, Mr. Larson, we'll get you to the main shore as soon as we can; that is, providing the lady who has hired this sloop is willing to go on without stopping here. I reckon this young man is your friend?"

"He is my son. And you are—?"

"Randy Fairwell, at your service, sir. It's too bad you were wrecked, but you can be thankful your life was spared. Seen anybody around here since you've been ashore?"

"Not a soul."

"Nor any sail?"

"Nothing. It has been very, very lonesome," and Arnold Baxter shook his head hypocritically.

Tom and Sam listened to this talk with keen interest. Tom now nudged his brother.

"This has gone far enough," he whispered. "Those men seem all right and I'm sure will prove our friends. I'm going to show myself."

"Wait till the Baxters go on board," replied Sam. "Otherwise they may take it into their heads to run away again."

A few words more followed between those on the sloop and the Baxters, and then the latter ran on the deck of the sloop by means of a plank thrown out for that purpose.

Then Tom came forward, stick in hand, and Sam followed.

"Hold those men!" he cried. "Don't let them get away from you!"

Of course the men on the sloop were much astonished, both by the boys' sudden appearance and by the words which were spoken.

"What's that?" called out Randy Fairwell.

"Those Rover boys!" ejaculated Arnold Baxter, and his face turned white.

"I said, Hold those men!" repeated Tom. "Don't let them get away from you."

"What for? Who are you?"

"Those fellows are rascals, and the father is an escaped prison-bird," put in Sam. "Hold them or they will run, sure."

"It's false," burst out Dan Baxter. "That fellow is crazy. I never saw him before."

"I guess they are both crazy," put in Arnold Baxter, taking the cue from his son. "Certainly I never set eyes on them before."

"Do not believe one word of what he says," said Tom. "His name is not what he said, but Arnold Baxter, and he is the man who got out of a New York prison by means of a forged pardon. You must have read of that case in the newspapers last summer?"

"I did read of it," answered Randy Fairwell. "But—but—" He was too bewildered to go on. "Where did you young men come from?"

"We were carried off in a schooner hired by these rascals and put in a cave on this island. We escaped only after a hard fight."

"But why were you carried off?" asked one of the other men on board of the sloop.

"These Baxters wanted to get our father to pay them money for our safe return."

"A kidnapping, eh?"

"It's a—a fairy story, and these fellows must be stark mad!" cried Arnold Baxter. "I give you my word, gentlemen, I never set eyes on the chaps before. Either they are escaped lunatics or else their lonely life here has turned their brains."

For a moment there was a pause; Sam and Tom standing at the end of the plank, clubs in hand, and the Baxters on the deck of the sloop, surrounded by the three men who had been sailing the craft. Those of the sloop looked from one party to the other in bewilderment.

"Well, I must say I don't know whom to believe," said Randy Fairwell slowly. He turned to the boys. "Who are you?"

"Tom Rover, and this is my brother Sam," answered the elder of the pair.

"I never heard the name before," said Arnold Baxter loftily.

"They don't appear to be very crazy," put in one of the men, whose name was Ruff.

"That's true, but they must be crazy or they wouldn't address my father and me in this fashion," said Dan Baxter.

"They can talk all they please," retorted Sam. "But if you let them escape, you will make a great mistake."

"Here is a fair suggestion," said Tom. "Take us all to the mainland and to the nearest police station. The authorities will soon straighten out this tangle."

"That certainly seems fair," muttered Randy Fairwell.

"I say these boys must be crazy," blustered Arnold Baxter. "If you take them on board, the chances are they'll try to murder us."

"I don't want to sail with a couple of crazy fellows," put in Dan, scowling darkly at the Rovers.

"We might keep a close watch on them," suggested Ruff.

"And keep a close watch on the Baxters," added Tom.

At this moment the door of the tiny cabin of the sloop opened, and a girl came out, rubbing her eyes as if she had been taking a nap, which was a fact.

She stared at the Baxters like one in a dream, and then gave a sudden cry of alarm.

"Is it you!"

"Dora Stanhope!" ejaculated Tom and Sam in a breath.

Then the girl started and turned her eyes ashore. "Tom Rover! And Sam! Where in the wide world did you come from?"

The Baxters fell back, almost overcome, and the father clutched the arm of his son savagely.

"We've put our foot into it here," he muttered.

"Who would have supposed that she was on this boat?" came from the son.

"Do you know these folks, Miss Stanhope?" questioned Randy Fairwell.

"Yes, I know all of them." answered the girl, when she had somewhat recovered from her surprise.

"Of course she knows us," put in Tom, "and she knows those rascals, too; don't you, Dora?"

"Yes, Tom. But how did you come here?"

"It's a long tale, Dora. But just now I want you to help me bring the Baxters to justice. They are trying to make out that they are all right and that we are crazy."

"Crazy! The idea! Indeed, Mr. Fairwell, these boys are not crazy. They are my best friends. They are Tom and Sam Rover, and they are brothers to the Dick Rover I told you about."

"And what of these fellows?" questioned the master of

the sloop.

"This man is an escaped prisoner, and this is his son, who is also wanted by the authorities, I believe."

"Trash and nonsense!" stormed Arnold Baxter, hardly knowing what to say. "This is simply a plot against us." He caught his son by the arm. "Come, we had better be going, since we are not wanted here."

He leaped upon the plank and Dan came after him.

"Get back there!" roared Tom, standing at the outer end of the plank. "Another step and I'll crack your head open, Arnold Baxter!"

And he swung his club in the air defiantly.

"Out of my way, or I will fire on you!" answered Arnold Baxter, and started to draw his pistol.

"Oh, don't!" screamed Dora, and covered her face with her hands.

"We want no shooting here—" began Randy Fairwell, and then stopped short in wonder.

For reaching down, Tom had suddenly given the end of the plank a wobble. Before they could save themselves, the Baxters, father and son, pitched with a loud splash into the lake.

"Good for you!" cried Sam. "If only they don't try to shoot when they come up."

There was a commotion in the water and mud lining the shore, and slowly the Baxters appeared to view, covered with slime and weeds, and both empty-handed, for Dan had not had time to draw his weapon, and that of the father lay somewhere on the bottom.

"Now do you surrender, or shall I do a little shooting?" said Tom sternly, although he had no weapon.

"Don't shoot me, please don't!" howled Dan, his last bit of courage deserting him.

The father said nothing, but looked as if he would like to annihilate both of the Rovers.

Randy Fairwell turned quickly to Dora Stanhope.

"You are certain these people are bad?" he said.

"Yes, yes; very bad!" answered Dora, and continued: "You can believe all the Rovers tell you concerning them."

One end of the plank still rested on the sloop, and Fairwell quickly placed the board in position again.

By this time the Baxters were crawling out of the lake. Sam caught hold of Dan while Tom tackled the father.

With a heavy boathook in his hand Randy Fairwell now ran ashore, followed by Ruff.

"You had better give up the fight," said Fairwell to Arnold Baxter. "If you are in the right, you shall have justice done to you."

"I will never give in!" growled Arnold Baxter savagely, and did his best to get away. Seeing this, Sam let Dan go and started in to help Tom. The struggle lasted several minutes, but Fairwell put an end to it by catching Arnold Baxter from behind and holding him in a grasp of iron, and then the rascal was made a close prisoner by being bound with a rope.

"Now for Dan!" cried Tom, and turned around, to find that Dan Baxter had taken time by the forelock and disappeared. It was destined to be many a day before any of the Rovers set eyes on him again.

CHAPTER XXX

HOME AGAIN—CONCLUSION

"Dan is gone!"

"Which way did he go?"

"I don't know."

"He ran up the shore, in that direction!" called out Dora, pointing with her hand.

Leaving Arnold Baxter in the grasp of Fairwell and Ruff, Tom and Sam hurried off.

But Dan Baxter had disappeared in a perfect wilderness of rocks and bushes and could not be located.

"Never mind," said Tom; "let him go, if he wants to remain on this lonely spot."

All were soon on board the sloop, and Tom and Sam told their tale, to which Dora, as well as the others, listened with close attention.

"Then my mother is safe!" burst out the girl. "Thank Heaven for that!"

Arthur M. Winfield

"She was safe when last we saw her," said Tom. "I guess the best thing we can do will be to get back to the wreck of the *Wellington* without delay."

"Yes! yes! take me to my mother at once. I have been hunting for her ever since she disappeared."

"But how did you happen to come here?"

"I found out that Josiah Crabtree had hired the *Wellington*, and day before yesterday we ran across a steamboat which had sighted the schooner headed in this direction."

"How did he get her away in the first place?"

"We were stopping at a hotel in Canada and I went out to do some necessary shopping. When I got back my mother was gone. She had received a bogus note, written I presume by Crabtree, asking her to come to me at once, as I had been taken sick in one of the stores. I immediately hired a detective, Mr. Ruff here, and we tracked Mr. Crabtree to the lake."

"Good for you, Dora,—a man couldn't have done better," cried Sam so enthusiastically that Dora had to blush.

"But now I want to get to mother without further delay."

"Let us set sail at once, then," said Tom. "The distance to the wreck is not over two miles."

Without delay the anchor was hoisted, the mainsail set, and the sloop left the shore. She was a trim-built craft, and under a good breeze her bow cut the shining waters of the lake like a knife.

The only one on the boat who was not in good humor was

Arnold Baxter. When he got the chance he called Tom Rover to him.

"Rover, what do you intend to do with me?" he asked.

"We intend to hand you over to the authorities."

"You are making a great mistake."

"I'll risk that."

"If you'll let me go I'll promise to turn over a new leaf, and, more than that, I'll help your father to make a pile of money out of that mine in Colorado."

"Your promises are not worth the breath they are uttered in, Arnold Baxter. You belong in prison, and that is where you are going."

At this Baxter began to rave and utter words unfit to print. But Tom soon stopped this.

"Keep a civil tongue in your head, or we'll gag you," he said, and then Baxter relapsed into sullen silence.

The breeze was favorable, and it was not long before the sloop rounded a point of the island and came in sight of the *Wellington*.

"Let us surprise old Crabtree," suggested Sam. "We can keep out of his sight until the last moment."

Tom was willing, yet Dora demurred, wishing to get to her mother as soon as possible. Yet, as they drew closer, the girl stepped behind the cabin for a minute.

"A ship!" cried Peglace, who was on watch on deck. "A ship

at last, and coming to shore!"

He uttered the words in French, and they speedily brought to the deck his companion and his companion's fat wife.

"A ship, sure enough," said the other Canadian, while his wife shed tears of joy.

Josiah Crabtree had just been interviewing Mrs. Stanhope in the cabin. He was trying again to hypnotize her, and she was trying to keep from under the spell.

"A boat must be coming, by the cries," said the former teacher. "I will go to the deck and investigate."

He ran up the companion way, and Mrs. Stanhope followed. The lady felt weak and utterly discouraged.

"If I only had Dora with me!" she murmured to herself.

"Did you speak?" asked Crabtree, looking over his shoulder.

"Not to you," she answered coldly.

Soon Crabtree was at the stern. The sloop came closer, and a rope was thrown to the *Wellington* and made fast by the Canadians. The smaller craft drew so little water that she did not ground, even when lying at the larger ship's stern.

"Hullo!" began Josiah Crabtree, addressing Randy Fairwell. "This is most fortunate."

"I see you are wrecked," returned Fairwell calmly.

"Exactly, sir—a very unfortunate affair truly. Will you rescue us?"

"Anybody else on board?"

"Yes, a lady to whom I am engaged to be married," and Crabtree smiled blandly. "Will you come on board?"

"I guess I will," answered Fairwell. "Eh, Mr. Ruff?"

"Yes," answered the detective, and leaped on the deck of the wreck.

By this time Mrs. Stanhope was on deck also, gazing curiously at those on the sloop.

"I believe this is Mr. Josiah Crabtree?" went on Ruff coldly.

"Eh? Why—er—you have the advantage of me!" stammered the former teacher of Putnam Hall, falling back in dismay.

"Are you Josiah Crabtree or not?"

"I am; but—"

"Then consider yourself my prisoner, Mr. Crabtree."

"Your prisoner!"

"That is what I said."

"But why do you say I am arrested? Who are you?"

"You are arrested for plotting against the welfare of Mrs. Stanhope there and Dora Stanhope, her daughter; also for forging Dora Stanhope's name to a letter sent to the girl's mother."

"It is false. I—I—Oh!"

Josiah Crabtree staggered back, for Dora had run forward. In a second more mother and daughter were in each other's arms. An affecting scene followed. Josiah Crabtree turned a sickly green, and his knees smote together.

"I—er—that is, we—the lady and myself—there is some mistake." He tried to go on, but failed utterly.

"You fraud, you!" cried Tom, and came forward, followed by Sam. "Now, Josiah Crabtree, we are on top, and we mean to stay there. Mr. Ruff, you had better handcuff him."

"I will," returned the detective, and brought forth a pair of steel "nippers."

"Handcuff me!" groaned Crabtree, "Oh, the disgrace! No! no!"

"You ought to have thought of the disgrace before," was Ruff's comment, and the next minute the handcuffs were fast on the prisoner.

A shout was now heard from one of the Canadian sailors. He was pointing to the north of the island, where a steam tug had just hove into sight.

The tug was coming on rapidly, and as she drew closer Tom and Sam made out a youth standing on the cabin top, eagerly waving his hand to them.

"Dick!" cried both of the Rovers. "Dick, by all that is wonderful!"

It was indeed Dick and the *Rocket*, and soon the steam tug came up to the stern of the sloop and made fast.

"Tom and Sam, and safe!" burst out Dick, and then his eyes

fell upon the Stanhopes. "Dora!" He shook hands and blushed deeply, and so did the girl. "Why, I never expected this!"

"None of us did," answered Dora with a warm smile.

"And your mother, too!"

"It's like a fairy tale," put in Tom, "and I guess it's going to end just as happily as fairy tales usually do."

It took some time for each to tell his story. When it came to Dick's turn, he said the steam tug had done her best to follow up Captain Langless and his schooner, but had failed because of the darkness.

"She's now out of sight," he concluded, "and there is no telling where she is."

"Well, let him go," said Tom. "We have Arnold Baxter, and he is the chief villain. I don't believe Captain Langless will ever bother us again."

After a long conversation it was decided that all of the party should return to the mainland in the steam tug and the sloop, the latter to be towed by the former. Dick remained on the sloop with the Stanhopes, while Josiah Crabtree was placed in the company of his fellow-criminal, Arnold Baxter. With the party went the Canadian who was married, and his wife, leaving the other Canadian to look after the wreck until his partner should return with material with which the boat could be patched up.

The run to the mainland was a pleasing one to the Rovers, and also to Larry and faithful Aleck Pop. The negro was on a broad grin over the safety of the brothers.

"Dem boys beat de nation," he said. "Nebber gits into trouble so deep but wot da paddles out ag'in in short ordah; yes, sah!"

During the trip it was decided by the Stanhopes, on Dick's advice, to prosecute Josiah Crabtree to the full extent of the law. Mrs. Stanhope demurred somewhat to this, but Dora was firm, and when the case was brought to trial Crabtree was sent to prison for two years.

The first thing the Rover boys did when on shore was to telegraph to their father, telling him of their safety. This telegram caught Mr. Rover just as he was about to arrange for sending the ten thousand dollars to Arnold Baxter. He was overjoyed at the glad tidings, and came on as far as Detroit to meet the whole party.

"My boys, how you must have suffered!" he said, as he shook one after another by the hand. "In the future you must be more careful!"

Arnold Baxter wished to see Anderson Rover, hoping thereby to influence the latter in his behalf, but Mr. Rover refused to grant the interview, and on the day following Arnold Baxter was sent back to the prison in New York State, there to begin his long term of imprisonment all over again.

There was much speculation concerning Dan Baxter, and when the Rovers went back to the island on the steam tug,—to obtain what had been discovered in the cave,— they asked the Canadian on the wreck if he had seen the youth.

"Yes, I see him," was the answer. "But he is gone now. He went off in a small boat that torched here yesterday."

"It's just as well," said Tom. "We didn't want to see the fellow starve here."

But at the cave which Dick and the others had discovered he changed his tune, for there were many signs that Dan Baxter had visited the locality. The money which had been lying on the dust-covered table was gone, likewise the map and the dagger.

"We are out that much," said Dick to Larry and Peterson.

"The boxes and casks are not disturbed," replied the old lumberman.

"He couldn't carry those," said Larry. "Perhaps he thinks to come back for these later."

"Then we'll fool him," replied Dick.

All of the goods were transferred to the steam tug and taken to Detroit, where, after remaining unclaimed for some time, they were sold, the sale netting the Rovers and their friends several thousand dollars.

One odd-shaped box Dick kept as a souvenir. It had been a money casket and was lined with brass. Little did the youth dream of all the strange adventures into which that casket was to lead him and his brothers. What those adventures were will be told in another volume of this series to be entitled, "THE ROVER BOYS IN THE MOUNTAINS; or, A HUNT FOR FUN AND FORTUNE."

The home-coming of the three boys was celebrated in grand style, not alone by the Covers, but by many of their friends, who flocked in from far and near to see them. Captain Putnam was there, along with many of their old schoolfellows.

Arthur M. Winfield

"It's good to be home once more," said Sam.

"Especially with so many friends around you," added Tom.

"And after escaping from so many perils," came from Dick.

And here let us leave them, wishing them well, both for the present and the future.

THE END

ABOUT THE AUTHOR

Edward Stratemeyer (October 4, 1862 - May 10, 1930). Born in Elizabeth, New Jersey he was an American publisher and writer of books for children. He created the Hardy Boys, Bobbsey Twins, Nancy Drew, Rover Boys, and Tom Swift series, among others.

Strameyer used a number of pen names, including Arthur M. Winfield. He wrote his first book and submitted to a publisher under this name which he is said to have chosen partly as a joke because it is a play on words, with "Arthur" being close to "author" and "Winfield" indicating his willingness to "win" and become famous as a children's book author.

Stratemeyer pioneered the technique of producing long-running, consistent series of books using a team of freelance authors to write standardized novels, which were published under a pen name owned by his company. Through his Stratemeyer Syndicate Stratemeyer produced short plot summaries for the novels in each series, which he sent to other writers who completed the story, writing a specified number of pages and chapters. Each book would begin with an introduction of the characters and would be interrupted at the first cliffhanger for a quick recap of all the previous books in the series.

Choose from Thousands of 1stWorldLibrary Classics By

A. M. Barnard
Ada Leverson
Adolphus William Ward
Aesop
Agatha Christie
Alexander Aaronsohn
Alexander Kielland
Alexandre Dumas
Alfred Gatty
Alfred Ollivant
Alice Duer Miller
Alice Turner Curtis
Alice Dunbar
Allen Chapman
Alleyne Ireland
Ambrose Bierce
Amelia E. Barr
Amory H. Bradford
Andrew Lang
Andrew McFarland Davis
Andy Adams
Angela Brazil
Anna Alice Chapin
Anna Sewell
Annie Besant
Annie Hamilton Donnell
Annie Payson Call
Annie Roe Carr
Annonaymous
Anton Chekhov
Archibald Lee Fletcher
Arnold Bennett
Arthur C. Benson
Arthur Conan Doyle
Arthur M. Winfield
Arthur Ransome
Arthur Schnitzler
Arthur Train
Atticus
B.H. Baden-Powell
B. M. Bower
B. C. Chatterjee
Baroness Emmuska Orczy
Baroness Orczy
Basil King
Bayard Taylor
Ben Macomber
Bertha Muzzy Bower
Bjornstjerne Bjornson

Booth Tarkington
Boyd Cable
Bram Stoker
C. Collodi
C. E. Orr
C. M. Ingleby
Carolyn Wells
Catherine Parr Traill
Charles A. Eastman
Charles Amory Beach
Charles Dickens
Charles Dudley Warner
Charles Farrar Browne
Charles Ives
Charles Kingsley
Charles Klein
Charles Hanson Towne
Charles Lathrop Pack
Charles Romyn Dake
Charles Whibley
Charles Willing Beale
Charlotte M. Braeme
Charlotte M. Yonge
Charlotte Perkins Stetson
Clair W. Hayes
Clarence Day Jr.
Clarence E. Mulford
Clemence Housman
Confucius
Coningsby Dawson
Cornelis DeWitt Wilcox
Cyril Burleigh
D. H. Lawrence
Daniel Defoe
David Garnett
Dinah Craik
Don Carlos Janes
Donald Keyhoe
Dorothy Kilner
Dougan Clark
Douglas Fairbanks
E. Nesbit
E. P. Roe
E. Phillips Oppenheim
E. S. Brooks
Earl Barnes
Edgar Rice Burroughs
Edith Van Dyne
Edith Wharton

Edward Everett Hale
Edward J. O'Biren
Edward S. Ellis
Edwin L. Arnold
Eleanor Atkins
Eleanor Hallowell Abbott
Eliot Gregory
Elizabeth Gaskell
Elizabeth McCracken
Elizabeth Von Arnim
Ellem Key
Emerson Hough
Emilie F. Carlen
Emily Bronte
Emily Dickinson
Enid Bagnold
Enilor Macartney Lane
Erasmus W. Jones
Ernie Howard Pie
Ethel May Dell
Ethel Turner
Ethel Watts Mumford
Eugene Sue
Eugenie Foa
Eugene Wood
Eustace Hale Ball
Evelyn Everett-green
Everard Cotes
F. H. Cheley
F. J. Cross
F. Marion Crawford
Fannie E. Newberry
Federick Austin Ogg
Ferdinand Ossendowski
Fergus Hume
Florence A. Kilpatrick
Fremont B. Deering
Francis Bacon
Francis Darwin
Frances Hodgson Burnett
Frances Parkinson Keyes
Frank Gee Patchin
Frank Harris
Frank Jewett Mather
Frank L. Packard
Frank V. Webster
Frederic Stewart Isham
Frederick Trevor Hill
Frederick Winslow Taylor

Friedrich Kerst
Friedrich Nietzsche
Fyodor Dostoyevsky
G.A. Henty
G.K. Chesterton
Gabrielle E. Jackson
Garrett P. Serviss
Gaston Leroux
George A. Warren
George Ade
Geroge Bernard Shaw
George Cary Eggleston
George Durston
George Ebers
George Eliot
George Gissing
George MacDonald
George Meredith
George Orwell
George Sylvester Viereck
George Tucker
George W. Cable
George Wharton James
Gertrude Atherton
Gordon Casserly
Grace E. King
Grace Gallatin
Grace Greenwood
Grant Allen
Guillermo A. Sherwell
Gulielma Zollinger
Gustav Flaubert
H. A. Cody
H. B. Irving
H.C. Bailey
H. G. Wells
H. H. Munro
H. Irving Hancock
H. R. Naylor
H. Rider Haggard
H. W. C. Davis
Haldeman Julius
Hall Caine
Hamilton Wright Mabie
Hans Christian Andersen
Harold Avery
Harold McGrath
Harriet Beecher Stowe
Harry Castlemon
Harry Coghill
Harry Houidini

Hayden Carruth
Helent Hunt Jackson
Helen Nicolay
Hendrik Conscience
Hendy David Thoreau
Henri Barbusse
Henrik Ibsen
Henry Adams
Henry Ford
Henry Frost
Henry James
Henry Jones Ford
Henry Seton Merriman
Henry W Longfellow
Herbert A. Giles
Herbert Carter
Herbert N. Casson
Herman Hesse
Hildegard G. Frey
Homer
Honore De Balzac
Horace B. Day
Horace Walpole
Horatio Alger Jr.
Howard Pyle
Howard R. Garis
Hugh Lofting
Hugh Walpole
Humphry Ward
Ian Maclaren
Inez Haynes Gillmore
Irving Bacheller
Isabel Cecilia Williams
Isabel Hornibrook
Israel Abrahams
Ivan Turgenev
J.G.Austin
J. Henri Fabre
J. M. Barrie
J. M. Walsh
J. Macdonald Oxley
J. R. Miller
J. S. Fletcher
J. S. Knowles
J. Storer Clouston
J. W. Duffield
Jack London
Jacob Abbott
James Allen
James Andrews
James Baldwin

James Branch Cabell
James DeMille
James Joyce
James Lane Allen
James Lane Allen
James Oliver Curwood
James Oppenheim
James Otis
James R. Driscoll
Jane Abbott
Jane Austen
Jane L. Stewart
Janet Aldridge
Jens Peter Jacobsen
Jerome K. Jerome
Jessie Graham Flower
John Buchan
John Burroughs
John Cournos
John F. Kennedy
John Gay
John Glasworthy
John Habberton
John Joy Bell
John Kendrick Bangs
John Milton
John Philip Sousa
John Taintor Foote
Jonas Lauritz Idemil Lie
Jonathan Swift
Joseph A. Altsheler
Joseph Carey
Joseph Conrad
Joseph E. Badger Jr
Joseph Hergesheimer
Joseph Jacobs
Jules Vernes
Julian Hawthrone
Julie A Lippmann
Justin Huntly McCarthy
Kakuzo Okakura
Karle Wilson Baker
Kate Chopin
Kenneth Grahame
Kenneth McGaffey
Kate Langley Bosher
Kate Langley Bosher
Katherine Cecil Thurston
Katherine Stokes
L. A. Abbot
L. T. Meade

L. Frank Baum
Latta Griswold
Laura Dent Crane
Laura Lee Hope
Laurence Housman
Lawrence Beasley
Leo Tolstoy
Leonid Andreyev
Lewis Carroll
Lewis Sperry Chafer
Lilian Bell
Lloyd Osbourne
Louis Hughes
Louis Joseph Vance
Louis Tracy
Louisa May Alcott
Lucy Fitch Perkins
Lucy Maud Montgomery
Luther Benson
Lydia Miller Middleton
Lyndon Orr
M. Corvus
M. H. Adams
Margaret E. Sangster
Margret Howth
Margaret Vandercook
Margaret W. Hungerford
Margret Penrose
Maria Edgeworth
Maria Thompson Daviess
Mariano Azuela
Marion Polk Angellotti
Mark Overton
Mark Twain
Mary Austin
Mary Catherine Crowley
Mary Cole
Mary Hastings Bradley
Mary Roberts Rinehart
Mary Rowlandson
M. Wollstonecraft Shelley
Maud Lindsay
Max Beerbohm
Myra Kelly
Nathaniel Hawthrone
Nicolo Machiavelli
O. F. Walton
Oscar Wilde

Owen Johnson
P.G. Wodehouse
Paul and Mabel Thorne
Paul G. Tomlinson
Paul Severing
Percy Brebner
Percy Keese Fitzhugh
Peter B. Kyne
Plato
Quincy Allen
R. Derby Holmes
R. L. Stevenson
R. S. Ball
Rabindranath Tagore
Rahul Alvares
Ralph Bonehill
Ralph Henry Barbour
Ralph Victor
Ralph Waldo Emmerson
Rene Descartes
Ray Cummings
Rex Beach
Rex E. Beach
Richard Harding Davis
Richard Jefferies
Richard Le Gallienne
Robert Barr
Robert Frost
Robert Gordon Anderson
Robert L. Drake
Robert Lansing
Robert Lynd
Robert Michael Ballantyne
Robert W. Chambers
Rosa Nouchette Carey
Rudyard Kipling
Saint Augustine
Samuel B. Allison
Samuel Hopkins Adams
Sarah Bernhardt
Sarah C. Hallowell
Selma Lagerlof
Sherwood Anderson
Sigmund Freud
Standish O'Grady
Stanley Weyman
Stella Benson
Stella M. Francis

Stephen Crane
Stewart Edward White
Stijn Streuvels
Swami Abhedananda
Swami Parmananda
T. S. Ackland
T. S. Arthur
The Princess Der Ling
Thomas A. Janvier
Thomas A Kempis
Thomas Anderton
Thomas Bailey Aldrich
Thomas Bulfinch
Thomas De Quincey
Thomas Dixon
Thomas H. Huxley
Thomas Hardy
Thomas More
Thornton W. Burgess
U. S. Grant
Upton Sinclair
Valentine Williams
Various Authors
Vaughan Kester
Victor Appleton
Victor G. Durham
Victoria Cross
Virginia Woolf
Wadsworth Camp
Walter Camp
Walter Scott
Washington Irving
Wilbur Lawton
Wilkie Collins
Willa Cather
Willard F. Baker
William Dean Howells
William le Queux
W. Makepeace Thackeray
William W. Walter
William Shakespeare
Winston Churchill
Yei Theodora Ozaki
Yogi Ramacharaka
Young E. Allison
Zane Grey

LaVergne, TN USA
03 February 2010
172032LV00001B/180/A